GRACE
WILL LEAD
YOU HOME

DR. NINA NELSON-GARRETT

Published by Mynd Matters Publishing
201 17th Street NW, Suite 300, Atlanta, GA 30363
www.myndmatterspublishing.com

Library of Congress Control Number: 2018907651
ISBN-13: 978-1-948145-07-7

FIRST EDITION

Printed in the United States of America

To my late parents,
Dr. M. K. Nelson and Mrs. Madeline Nelson

CHAPTER 1

"**D**r. Grace Wilson-Livingston, please call extension eight-seven-seven-six, stat! Dr. Wilson-Livingston, please call the ICU, stat!" said a hospital operator on the overhead speaker as Grace entered from the physician's parking garage at 6:45 a.m.

A petite, forty-four-year-old African-American woman, Grace looked down as she felt the humming of her pager and heard two consecutive beeps, alerting her to an urgent need. The numbers 865-555-3212-911 stared back at her. She called the ICU from her cellphone and spoke with a frantic gastroenterology fellow.

"Good morning Dr. Livingston, I'm McKinley Steele, the first-year GI fellow who's been on call overnight. I got a call about twenty minutes ago about a patient in ICU bed seven," said Dr. Steele.

Throwing her head back, Grace asked, "What makes this call so urgent that I have gotten overhead pages and a 911 sent on my beeper?"

"I'm sorry, but he's an elderly man passing a lot of foul-smelling blood. I think he's going to need an emergency endoscopy this morning."

Feeling her heart racing and her blood pressure rising, Grace asked, "Is the blood black or bright red? Is he throwing up blood or only passing blood in the stool?"

"Oh, I'm sorry, ma'am, he threw up bright red blood and passed several black bowel movements. Also, his blood pressure is really low. I ordered two units of blood and asked the nurses to place two large bore IV lines."

"Okay, I'm already in the hospital and am almost at the ICU," said Grace calmly. "Did you call the endoscopy team to get them to the bedside? Also, I forgot to ask—is he on any blood thinners?"

"Oh yes, ma'am, I've already called the endoscopy team, and they're on their way. And no blood thinners."

"Okay, I'll be there shortly."

As she arrived at the ICU, she scanned her badge over the sensor outside the door that allowed her entry. Just as she stepped inside the doorway, her pager sounded again. She looked at it as she walked over to bed seven. She grunted and nodded to the first-year GI fellow who looked like he had seen a ghost.

"Hi, Dr. Steele, I'm not sure we've worked together before. I think I've seen you in passing in the department."

"No, ma'am, I haven't worked with you yet."

"Okay, so how many endoscopies have you done so far this year, Dr. Steele?"

"Oh, maybe thirty-five or so."

"Well, given the complexity of this case and your procedure numbers, I'll do this procedure because this patient is pretty sick. You can just watch."

She noticed that his left eye stopped twitching as he said, "That's not a problem at all, ma'am. I was a little worried about having to do such a complex case at this stage of my training, anyway."

Grace's pager squealed again. She looked down. "Are you kidding me? It's too early for this! Why is the operator calling me repeatedly?"

Just as she was about to pick up the phone at the nurses' station, the endoscopy team arrived. She followed them to the patient's room as she prepared to perform an examination on a pale, debilitated elderly gentleman. She asked the patient questions about his symptoms and listened as he described being short of breath when he tried to walk.

Dr. Steele added, "I forgot to tell you that he told me about a history of stomach ulcers several years ago and that he's been taking a lot of ibuprofens for arthritis pain."

Grace nodded as she moved her stethoscope over the old man's chest and abdomen.

"Did you review the procedure and the risks with the patient Dr. Steele?" she asked as she gloved and gowned to perform the endoscopy.

"Yes, I did, and he signed the consent."

"Great, let's get started."

She passed the endoscope and found a large gastric ulcer with a spurting artery at the base. After performing multiple hemostatic procedures, each of which Grace explained to the GI fellow as to how and why it was done, she was able to control the bleeding.

Once the endoscopy was finished, she called the operator.

"This is Dr. Wilson-Livingston. Did you call?"

The operator said, "Yes ma'am, one of your associate's patients has been calling repeatedly about needing a pain medication prescription."

"Tell the patient that he needs to call the office during normal business hours! The office will be open in about twenty minutes. I don't prescribe pain meds based on phone conversations anyway," barked Grace.

"Yes ma'am, I'm sorry. I'm just doing my job," stated the operator.

"I know. It's just been an eventful morning already," said Grace.

She hung up the phone, turned to the GI fellow, and asked him to finish up the paperwork because she was already late for morning rounds.

She heaved a sigh and headed to the gastroenterology unit. Upon her arrival, the GI ward team was already assembled. The team consisted of a different GI fellow, a second-year resident, and a fourth-year medical student.

"Hi, guys. I'm sorry I'm late, but I had an emergency in the ICU," she said as she smiled at the team.

The second-year resident said, "We heard about that case. Is the patient okay?"

"He's stable but not completely out of the woods. All right, let's get moving."

As they walked into a patient's room, she turned to the fourth-year medical student and asked, "So, can you give me the differential diagnosis for why this patient's liver enzymes are elevated?"

To which the fourth-year student answered, "Ah, let's see. Could it be hepatitis?"

"Yes, it definitely could be hepatitis, but hepatitis is a general term that simply means inflammation of the liver. I need you to dig deeper when thinking about this patient's care. I want you to give me a five-minute presentation tomorrow about why elevated liver enzymes occur." Teaching was one of her favorite things to do.

As Grace finished morning rounds, she received a text message reminding her that a mandatory gastroenterology department meeting was about to start. Dr. Hank Malloy, the chief of the department, had been planning to announce changes in positions for the faculty, which made Grace edgy. Today was a big day. She had wanted the clinical director of fellowship position for a while. Even if it meant more paperwork and time consumption, she was up for the task.

Heels clicking down the hall, she rushed to the front of the hospital to exit down the steps and cross the road to the clinic building.

As she approached the steps, she lost her footing. She plunged forward and bumped her chest on the edge of one step, her left knee dragging across another step. Face flushing, she winced. Two nurses and a few hospital visitors rushed over to help. As she picked herself up, she wondered if this was an omen about the meeting.

"Are you okay? Do you need to go to the emergency room?" asked a nurse who assisted her in standing.

"I'm fine. Please just leave me alone. It's really no big deal. I only scraped my knee for Christ's sake," she snapped.

By the time she arrived at the gastroenterology conference room, five floors up from the entrance of the medical clinic, all twenty-two physicians in the gastroenterology department had arrived and were seated around a large conference table, and she was late.

Dr. Malloy stood at a large dry erase board at the front of the room, mapping out the changes that he planned for the department.

He glanced down at his watch.

"I'm glad to see that you were able to join us, Dr. Livingston."

Grace forced a smile, but her bleeding knee was visible to all, which made her uncomfortable and caused Dr. Malloy to recoil a bit.

"Are you okay?" he asked. "Do you need to go clean that up?"

"No, I'm fine. Just a small accident," said Grace.

Her heart pounded as she thought about her bruised knee and ego.

With a nod, Dr. Malloy continued. "The university is going through a restructuring process. There has been a call for more diversity in leadership roles. I have decided to make a few changes in division positions based on levels of competency, dedication to the department, as well as a need for new ways of thinking as we move forward. This is in no way a slight to some of our more senior faculty members, but I think it will be best if we rotate these leadership roles every few years or so. I want everyone to be fully engaged."

He began detailing in writing the upcoming changes. First, he wrote Dr. Sims's name as the new director of the liver division and Dr. Moss as the director of endoscopy. Then he wrote *Dr. Wilson-Livingston.*

He turned to Grace and said, "You are the new clinical director of the fellowship program."

Her pain forgotten, Grace smiled. Finally! She had always wanted that position as it would allow her to have more interaction with the GI fellows. But after hearing her name, she stopped listening. Nothing seemed to matter after that. She just wanted to get home and tell her husband, Stewart, about the good news. So, she smiled and nodded.

After the meeting ended, she headed to the medical clinic for her afternoon office hours. Grace entered through the back door of the clinic and headed to her office without speaking to anyone. She closed the door and pulled out a first aid kit from a drawer and tended to her knee, cleaning it with an antiseptic wipe and placing a large bandage over it. Scrounging through her drawers, she found a bottle of acetaminophen and took two. She then looked at her afternoon schedule left on her desk by her assistant. She cringed when she saw that her first patient was an elderly woman who often got under her skin because she was so long-winded.

When Grace entered the exam room, the patient asked her usual question, "How's life treating you, doctor?"

"If it's not one thing, it's another," Grace answered.

The patient furrowed her brows, "Why do you do that? You say that a lot. That response is self-defeating."

Grace tried to hide her anger, but the best she could manage was a half-hearted smile as she said, "Because that's how I feel about today."

Grace knew she hadn't done a good job of hiding her emotions and was about to apologize, when the patient pulled a book from her purse by Norman Vincent Peale on the power of positive thinking. She held it out to Grace. Grace thanked her and decided it was time to get the woman out the office before anything else could be said. After she completed the physical exam, she walked her to the checkout window and then headed back to her office. She dropped the book on her desk firmly. *Some people take entirely too much liberty when they have no right. Who is she to tell me that I need to read a self-help book?*

While gathering her belongings at the end of her work day, she accidentally knocked the Norman Vincent Peale book onto the floor. The cover flipped open and she noticed a handwritten inscription from the patient, which read:

Dear Doctor,

Having a constructive and positive outlook requires constant positive influences and the use of affirming language and visuals. I hope this book helps you get there, because you are special to me and so many others. I want you to be happy and healthy.

She closed the book and sat it back on her desk as she ran her hand across the cover.

When she got home that night, she discussed her hectic day with Stewart.

She was surprised when all he said was, "I guess I should say congratulations about the promotion?" Then, without waiting for a response, he asked, "So, did you have someone take a look at your knee like the nurse suggested? It looks swollen."

"No, but I plan to soak it in the tub tonight. It'll be fine. Wow, that's all you have to say?"

"Yup, that's all I have to say, superwoman," he said, walking away. "You need some time away from that job."

CHAPTER 2

Three weeks later, wearing gray nylon sweatpants and a lime-green t-shirt, Grace stood in front of her recently purchased stainless steel range, relishing in the fact that she had finally gotten a day off work. She looked around, thinking about the things she would try to accomplish. Bending down slightly to turn two red knobs to the right, she ignited soft Carolina blue gas flames on the back burners. She smiled inwardly as she celebrated remembering which knob worked for what burner. Grace straightened up and let out a deep cough which had been plaguing her for a couple of weeks. She reached over to the coffee maker on the counter near the stove and pressed start, waiting for the steaming water to drip in regular gurgles over her peppermint tea bag dangling in her cup. After the cup was full, she placed a saucer over its lid and turned her attention to the task at hand, a surprise hot breakfast for her family. After which she would have a brief gym workout and then do a little shopping.

She placed a black sauce pot on a burner and filled it with water from the pot filler faucet on the wall behind the stove. She put a cup of grits in the water, turned the flame to a low burn, and then sealed the pot with a glass lid. She fried several strips of turkey bacon until it was glistening brown and crispy. Saving the eggs for last, she reached for her tea, uncovered her vaporous libation, and spooned in two teaspoons of honey. After blowing the surface of the tea for a few seconds, Grace felt the warmth of the liquid passing her throat and radiating across her chest. The soothing sensation seemed to be a quick fix for her cough. The phone rang and she answered on the second ring.

"Good morning Dr. Livingston, it's Alice," said the caller.

"Hi, Alice," said Grace.

"I was just checking with you to be sure you don't need me to come by the house and take the kids to school. I'm so used to being over there that I got up and started getting dressed before I remembered you gave me the day off."

"Thanks but no help needed. I'm in the process of cooking breakfast now."

"Okay, just checking. What about picking them up and getting them settled in after school?"

"Nope, I'm okay on that front, too. I'm going to act like a real parent today," said Grace, laughing.

"Okay, call if you need me."

"Will do, but please enjoy your day."

Grace placed the cordless phone back into its waiting cradle and returned to making breakfast.

As she spooned fluffy white grits, turkey bacon, and softly scrambled golden eggs onto royal blue plates that sat in stark contrast to the white marble countertops, she heard the squeaking of well-worn tennis shoes barreling down the hallway toward the kitchen, signaling that the day's activities had truly begun. Her children, Patrice and Christopher, barged through the doorway with backpacks in tow.

Nine-year-old Chris placed his backpack on the arm of a chair at the kitchen table. He crossed the room, sniffing the aromas as he came toward his mom.

"Man, breakfast smells good. I'm hungry," he said as he gave her a hug.

"I just finished cooking and it's piping hot. Grab your plate," Grace encouraged.

Chris did just that with thirteen-year-old Patrice following close behind. Patrice was wearing a pleated khaki skirt, a yellow Peter Pan collared shirt, and a navy-blue cardigan brandishing her school's logo. She picked up her plate and returned to the table without saying a word.

"Good morning, Patrice. Did you sleep okay?" Grace asked. "You're a bit antisocial this morning."

"No, I'm fine. I just don't feel like talking, that's all," Patrice said curtly.

"Oh, I see. Well, I hope your day gets better," said Grace. Then she turned to Chris.

"Can you believe it? I have a day off. So, while you guys are at school, I am going to the gym and then I plan to do some early Christmas shopping."

Chris looked up from his plate barely able to contain his excitement. "Can I please go with you? My teacher won't mind if I miss school today." Egg flew from his overfilled mouth as he spoke.

"Your teacher may not mind, but I certainly do. Besides, since when have I ever allowed you to miss school to go shopping? I think I'm capable of reading your lists and getting the things you guys want," Grace said as her voice trailed off. Patrice looked away and grunted under her breath.

At almost the same moment, Grace heard heavier pigeon-toed footsteps coming down the hallway. Stewart entered the kitchen with a giant smile and raised eyebrows. He stood tall in his six-foot-two-inch frame, wearing a tan blazer with navy pants, a white shirt, and a gold tie. He made his way to the stove, leaned in, and kissed Grace softly on the cheek.

"You look amazing," Grace murmured.

"Thanks babe," Stewart responded. "I need you to stay home more often. I get compliments and breakfast. If a day away from that mad house job of yours is all it takes to get your domestic diva side to come out, I'm going to call and say that you are sick tomorrow. You do have had that nagging cough after all."

Grace laughed. "Cute, but seriously, do you have to look this good to go to work? Tell those ladies at your office to keep their hands and eyes to themselves or else."

She handed Stewart a plate of food which he took to his usual spot at the table.

"I'll be sure to tell the ladies that they have been duly warned by my tough, five-foot-two wife," he said with a smile.

Grace winked to affirm his decision.

"I have a new client coming in today. If all goes well, it will be a nice marketing account for the office. So, I've got to put on my game face," said Stewart.

Then he turned his attention to the children and said, "Good morning, guys. Are you ready for an award-winning day?"

"I hope so," Chris responded as Stewart barely finished his statement.

Patrice didn't respond as she thumbed through text messages on her cell phone. Stewart asked her again, but

Patrice still didn't answer. Stewart dropped his fork and pushed his chair back.

"Listen young lady. When I speak, I need you to respond. Do you hear me? Please, turn that phone off!"

"I heard you. I already told mom that I don't feel like talking," Patrice snapped.

"Well, your fingers must feel like talking because they're moving a mile a minute on that phone!" said Stewart.

Patrice rolled her eyes and said sarcastically, "Mom said she is going to get Christmas gifts today. *She* said that she didn't need us to go with her because she couldn't *possibly* mess up getting gifts."

Stewart turned toward Grace who had her back to them as she stood at the kitchen sink.

"Mom told me about her plans earlier, but what's up with your disrespectful tone?" Stewart demanded. "And I think it's good that Mom has some free time to herself to get a few things done. She works so hard all of the time."

He looked back over his shoulder and asked, "Are you sure you don't need any help with anything, Grace?"

Grace raised her left brow and turned to face him with a plastered grin on her face. "I've got this, okay?" She glanced over at Patrice and then began mindlessly clearing dishes from the table.

Chris spouted, "Patrice, stop being mean to mom. You're always so rude."

His reproof was followed by a squeal as he said, "Mom, I'm not finished eating," pulling his plate out of Grace's hand.

"Sorry buddy. I was just a bit distracted by our conversation."

Grace then returned to the white farmhouse double sink with a stack of dishes. She rinsed them in one side of the sink as she filled the other side with hot, soapy water. Looking down into the frothy water, she became lost in her thoughts.

She knew she had let her family down the previous year by being so absorbed in her work. The ethics committee that she had been chairing at The University of Tennessee hospital had been bogged down in a case that involved a pregnant, mentally handicapped girl suffering from severe preeclampsia. The patient's family had demanded that no medications be given for religious reasons, despite knowing the girl could die. The case made the local news, throwing the hospital administration into an uproar, leading to what Grace felt were misguided frustrations directed at her. At that time, Grace was trying to manage family life, along with being a faculty member in the gastroenterology department of the university, as well as serving on several hospital committees. Frequent meetings, which often ran late into the night, consumed her time. She thought about how Christmas seemed to appear out of nowhere last year and she was woefully unprepared.

No repeats this year, she thought. No Christmas shopping at 9:30 p.m. on Christmas Eve for her family's gifts this year. Grace shuddered when she thought about how she bought boxes of chocolate-covered cherries, a snow globe with Mickey Mouse jousting Goofy, two sweatshirts with Rudolph's nose shining brightly, and several puzzles from a rack, labeled *After Christmas Sale* from the local drugstore as the store manager announced that the store would be closing in fifteen minutes. The memory of poor Stewart receiving a dark blue tie with yellow stars and a coffee mug adorned with a Christmas tree left her with a hollow sensation in her gut. She had hoped her family would offer her a pass on the oversight since she had been so busy with her work.

But standing at the sink, she relived the sadness on their faces as she looked up and out of the large, rectangular picture window over the sink. Patrice had deemed it the "suckiest Christmas ever." *I definitely let them down.*

Grace looked back over her shoulder and forced a smile as she said, "You guys are going to be late. Patrice, can you go and get my purse off of the bench in my room? I'll drop you both off at school."

"Umm, okay," Patrice said. "Why isn't Alice here?"

"I gave her the day off. Sorry, you're stuck with me. I hope you can handle that for one day."

Patrice walked away shaking her head as she said, "It's just that I was going to ask her about something."

"Well you can ask me. Maybe I can answer your question."

"No, I've been talking with Alice about something for a while. It can wait until I see her."

Stewart walked over to Grace and rubbed her back. "That child is driving me nuts. I know you keep saying she's a teenager and her hormones are making her crazy, but I don't get her sometimes."

"You need to get to work. Did you finish your breakfast?"

"I'm good. I've had enough to eat so I'm gonna head out."

"Look baby, I'm okay when it comes to Patrice. I've talked with a couple of female colleagues who have daughters about her age and based on their horror stories, it would appear we have a normal thirteen-year-old girl. I know Patrice and I seem to clash a lot these days, but we'll both get over it."

"I'm happy you have a rational mind right now because she really is driving me bonkers," countered Stewart as he kissed Grace on the forehead.

CHAPTER 3

As Grace scurried everyone out of the house, she pressed the button on her remote car key to unlock the doors of her SUV. The children climbed in, with Patrice claiming the front seat.

"Seatbelts fastened?"

"Yes ma'am," replied Chris.

"Uh-huh," mumbled Patrice as she scrolled through her phone.

As Grace distractedly buckled her own seatbelt, her mind floated to the memory of that previous Christmas. *Suckiest Christmas EVER* rang in her head. She recalled Stewart yelling at Patrice and saying that something like the word suck should never come out of her mouth in that context ever again. She remembered poor Christopher sitting in a corner asking if Santa got his letter and Patrice's painful rebuttal, "There is no Santa, dummy. Mom was supposed to buy our things, but she didn't. She was too busy at work, as usual."

Grace recalled Stewart snapping his fingers quickly in response to Patrice's comment and pointing in the direction of the hallway, sending her to her room. Chris had cried while she rubbed his back and tried to explain that she had made a mistake and blew it. She could still see his eyes filled with tears as he asked why Patrice was so mean to him and why she would say that about Santa.

"Mom, it's cold out here. Could you please start the car?" Patrice bellowed, bringing her out of her reveries.

"Oh, sorry, I thought I had," replied Grace as she choked back a cough.

After a short drive, Grace pulled into the school drop off lane.

"Patrice, I need you to think about how you plan to apologize to Dad tonight when he gets home. You have all day to think about it. Your funky attitude has got to go, okay?"

"Sure, whatever," said Patrice dismissively.

"Whatever? Whatever!" replied Grace. "See, that's what I'm talking about. You were raised with better manners than that. Give me your cellphone and you won't get it back for the rest of the week."

"Mom, you're not being fair. I need my phone!"

"Give me the phone and work on your attitude today!"

Patrice slapped her phone into Grace's palm and exited the car, slamming the door.

Grace then turned to Chris and said, "Remember, an award-winning day is what you're aiming for, buddy."

"Yes ma'am," said Chris.

Grace sat for a couple of seconds and shook her head as she thought about the fact that she hadn't a clue about how to deal with Patrice's mood changes despite what she had told Stewart earlier. After pulling out of the of school's traffic, Grace headed for Rocky Heights Gym.

She turned into the parking lot just before eight and unloaded her gym bag, which she always kept in the back of the SUV.

"Hey, Dr. Livingston, you're here early today," said a muscular twenty-something-year old standing at the front desk.

"Yeah, I have the day off. I'm trying to get in a short workout before doing some shopping."

"Cool."

After laying her gym card on the scanner, she waited for the ping and the glowing fluorescent green light on the device to signify her acceptance. She went to the ladies' locker room and changed into her running shorts and a tank top.

As she exited the changing room, she eyed the various types of exercise equipment. She walked past the elliptical machines and the free weights to step onto the first available treadmill. She set the speed at 4.5 mph and a level three incline, but within a few minutes had to slow it down to 3.0 mph and lower the incline to zero. She managed to keep up with that pace but noticed that her heart rate was fifteen points higher than usual. At the thirty-five-minute mark, she hit the cool down button and stepped off the treadmill, feeling her knees buckle and sweat rolling down her face. *This makes no sense. I can usually run twice as long and not feel like this.*

Once inside the ladies' locker room, she got a mesh body scrubber from her backpack and a towel for drying. After undressing, she went to the first unoccupied shower and turned on the hot water. After testing the temperature with her fingertips, she slowly stepped into the warm shower. But, in what seemed like a few seconds, the water pressure began to lower. Frustrated by what she felt was poor management, she wondered if Rocky Heights was working on getting its clients to leave fast and not loiter. *I pay far too much for a membership for this kind of service.* As she let the water fall over her head, she washed her hair and then wiped her soapy hands over her body. She stopped at her right breast.

"Hmmm, that feels like a lump," she said aloud.

She raised her arm and continued to palpate, hoping she was not feeling what was there. *Where did that come from? I don't remember feeling that before.* At that moment, the incident from three weeks prior popped into her head. *I bet I have a hematoma from that stupid fall.*

Grace turned off the water, stepped out of the shower, and toweled off. She kept coming back to the lump in her breast, thinking about how stupid she felt after she had fallen. I sure know how to get people's attention, she thought as she pulled her olive-green dress over her head and pulled on a pair of designer ankle boots. After dressing, she stood in front of a small mirror in the door of her locker as she combed through her wet hair and smoothed it back with hair gel before tying it up in what she called the perfect messy bun.

Grace stuffed her clothes and sneakers into her gym bag. Stopping again at the front desk on her way out, she told the manager about how dissatisfied she was with the problem she had while showering. She was assured that the matter would be addressed but doubted it since the manager failed to show genuine concern. She left the gym and headed for the mall.

CHAPTER 4

It was an unusually cool October day, less than a month before Thanksgiving, and the stores in Knoxville were already geared up for Christmas. Grace decided to be the ultimate consumer. Finding the must-have Christmas gifts was of the utmost importance. She also had a few other household items that were on her list.

Christopher told her several times that he couldn't live without a red Nintendo DS with silver letters, the Mario Box Kart game, and a Celestron PowerSeeker Telescope. Patrice was less vocal about her desires but no less wishful. She wanted a Vida sewing machine that could also do embroidery and an iPhone 5. Grace raised her eyebrows when she thought about the phone request and how ironic it was that Patrice's current cell phone was being held hostage in her purse. She considered playing hardball with Patrice about her attitude and her desire for a new phone. But, when Grace thought about their disastrous previous Christmas, she let that consideration evaporate.

Grace drove to the Turtle Creek Mall and went into several stores, buying gifts for her family as well as some of her co-workers. After about two hours of shopping, she thought that the bigger items the kids wanted would most likely be at Target. So, she loaded her purchased items into the back of the SUV and headed there. With the events of last year still fresh in her mind, she said to herself that this year she wanted her family to have a fabulous Thanksgiving and an amazing Christmas.

She pulled into the Target parking lot and parked near the door because her feet had begun to ache somewhat from her shoes. Surprisingly, the parking lot was fairly full. *Looks like everyone had the same idea as I did today.* As she exited the car, she bumped her previously injured knee on the edge of the door and gritted her teeth from the pain.

As Grace entered the automatic doors, a sensation of breathlessness overtook her. She pulled a large red plastic buggy out of the line of carts and realized that her breathing was labored as she started to cough again. A few beads of sweat popped up on her upper lip and forehead. *I cannot believe how tired I am.* She stopped at the Starbucks counter and picked up a grande caramel Frappuccino®. She hoped the caffeine would give her a much-needed boost of energy. She sipped on her frosty drink as she moved up and down the aisles of the store.

As she walked past the athletics department, she smiled and thought about a conversation she had with Chris a few weeks before when she had returned a kicked soccer ball he'd sent her way during his soccer practice.

"Wow, Mommy, that was a good kick. You're quick for your age, I mean, because you're forty-four," Chris had innocently shared. "You kick better than Kenny's mom and I know she's much younger than you are."

"Ouch, you know how to cut a girl."

"Cut a girl?" Chris said with a look of total bewilderment.

"That just means you're very honest and straightforward. I know I'm about ten years older than your friends' moms, but did you have to say it like that?"

Noting that he was still puzzled, she just said, "Thanks."

She leisurely strolled from the athletics department to electronics where she encountered a salesman.

"Excuse me, sir, can you tell me where I can find a red Nintendo 3DS and video games for it?" Grace asked.

"I sure can," an amiable silver-haired man responded.

Grace followed him to a glass case and watched him pull out a set of keys attached a retractable faded blue plastic wrist coil with a key ring. He unlocked a sliding door security lock for a glass case housing various coveted video games.

"Thank you. This is exactly what I was looking for."

She sat her frappe in the child carry seat of the cart and reached for the Mario Box Cart game. However, the salesman quickly blocked her hand as he said, "Uh, sorry, ma'am. I have to get it for you. The store prefers that we handle the games and not the customers."

"Oh, I see," said Grace. "The Fort Knox of video games, eh?" she laughed.

"Something like that. It's because people steal them so much. I don't understand it. That game you were reaching for is real popular."

After he secured the game, Grace pointed to two other popular games that she decided to purchase. The Nintendo DS was liberated from a different locked glass case.

Grace then asked him about the iPhone 5. She followed a few steps behind him as he led her to another aisle. After arriving at the display case, she hesitantly picked up a white iPhone 5s connected to a silver metal cable cord and scanned the features written on panel attached to the display holder. Though she wasn't completely comfortable with the purchase, she selected the white iPhone for Patrice.

Before leaving the counter, she asked the salesman, "Is that iPad Mini really only $125.00? Is there something wrong with it?"

"That's the right price. As far as I know, they're fine. But to tell you the truth, I don't know a lot about this stuff. I can call for someone else if you need me to," answered the salesman.

"That won't be necessary. I'll buy two of them. My kids will really be surprised when they see this."

"Is there anything else I can show you?"

"No, sir, I think I've done enough damage," Grace said with a smile.

"You'll have to pay for all of these things at the front of the store because these registers aren't working back here today. But, if you have some more shopping to do, I'll need to hold them until you get ready to check out."

"Sure, I have a few other items I need to get. So, do I just tell the front clerk to call you or do I have to come back here so that we can go up front together?"

"No ma'am, you can just have her call me back here and I'll bring them up."

Grace pushed her cart away from the counter and headed for the grocery section and picked up paper towels, toilet paper, napkins, eggs, milk, laundry detergent, cleaning supplies, and small stocking stuffer Christmas gifts. She finished the last sip of her drink while waiting in line for her final checkout but still felt tired, though jittery.

As Grace moved to the conveyor belt and unloaded her basket, she looked into the face of a very thin, fragile-looking blonde female cashier. She had talked to her many times in the past when she visited the store.

"I have several items from the electronics department that I need to purchase. The salesman asked me to have you call him."

"Yes ma'am, I'll call right now." It only took a couple of minutes for him to appear at the register with all of Grace's items. The young lady began scanning everything.

"Are you doing your Christmas shopping already?" she asked.

"What made you ask me that, Lauren? Your name is Lauren, right?" Grace asked hesitantly.

Lauren smiled, pointed to her name tag, and said, "You're right. It's just that you bought so many electronics. Your kids are lucky to have you as their mom."

"Thanks," Grace responded through repeated deep coughs. *If only you had been at my house last year, you would think otherwise.*

"Are you okay?" Lauren asked.

"I'm fine, just a little tired. I guess I'm not as young as I used to be, right?" Grace chuckled.

"Oh, you look great," responded Lauren.

CHAPTER 5

After rearranging items in the SUV, Grace sat in the driver's seat and looked at her watch. It was close to one thirty in the afternoon, so she headed for the freeway toward home. Merging into the traffic, she decided to drop off her packages at the house. She opened the door from the garage, walked through the mud room, and dropped her purse on the countertop in the kitchen. Although she was exhausted, she proceeded to unload the car. After stacking most of the Christmas items in her closet, she placed the household items in their appropriate places. She then took her cell phone from her purse and set her phone alarm for 3:00 p.m. She lay on the sofa in the family room to take a much-needed nap. Her coughing resurged which led her to reach for a peppermint from a candy dish on the sofa table. She fell asleep quickly with the mint dissolving and soothing her tickled throat.

At exactly 3:30 p.m., she pulled up to Well's Academy to pick up Patrice and Chris. The student pick up lane was off to the right of the main driveway into the school. She saw Chris standing on the grass near the pickup/drop off sign. She stopped, placed the car in park, but kept it running.

"Can I ride up front?" Chris asked as he opened the front passenger door and leaned in.

"You sure can," Grace replied.

Chris plowed into the car after putting his backpack on the back seat. Before he could get seated, he gave Grace a huge kiss and asked, "So, how did your shopping go today? I thought about it all day. Did you find everything I asked for?"

"Boy, get in the car and buckle your seatbelt. Where is Patrice? She knew I was supposed to be here at 3:30, and yes, I got everything I was supposed to get today," Grace laughed.

"I saw Patrice with some of her friends at the soda machine. She doesn't talk to me at school but she probably knows you're here. She can see you out of that window over there." Chris pointed to a large window near the gymnasium.

Grace dialed Patrice's number and then remembered that she had taken her cell phone from her that morning. She drummed her fingers on the steering wheel, looking down at her watch repeatedly as minutes continued to pass.

"Why does this child challenge me so much?" Grace mumbled under her breath.

"What? I didn't hear you," Chris asked as he turned the radio dial.

"I'm sorry, buddy. I was talking to myself."

Just as the last word was leaving her mouth, Patrice opened the back door to the car and asked, "Why does he get to sit up front? I'm the oldest."

"He got here before you. Where were you, anyway? I told you I'd be here at three thirty."

"It's only three forty-five mom, what's the big deal? I needed to talk with my friends about something," Patrice said in an irritated tone.

"The big deal is that when I tell you to be somewhere, I expect you to be there. My time is as valuable as yours—no, it's more valuable than yours!" Grace replied but felt herself gasp for air. She took that to be her sign to end what would likely become a seesaw conversation with Patrice.

The car quieted until Chris asked, "Can I listen to Radio Disney?"

"Not a problem," Grace said.

"What's for dinner?" Chris asked as he hummed the theme to *Beauty and the Beast*.

"I think tonight is a spaghetti and salad night. What do you think?" Grace asked.

"That sounds good."

"What about you, Patrice? Does spaghetti sound good?" Grace queried.

"Sure, that's fine," she responded curtly.

When they arrived home, Grace immediately took on the task of preparing dinner. She took the ground turkey out of the refrigerator that had been thawing all day and got a jar of organic spaghetti sauce from the pantry. She grabbed a large nonstick sauté pan from the white maple pull drawer cabinet below the stove. She placed a wooden cutting board on the countertop near the cooktop and asked Patrice to chop up fresh basil, thyme, oregano, onions, and bell peppers.

"If you turn on the vent over the stove, you may keep from crying while chopping those onions Patrice," Grace mentioned.

"Yes, ma'am." *She sounds like she's out of her funk for now. Let's see how long this lasts.*

Grace placed extra virgin olive oil in the pan and browned the turkey and then added all of the chopped ingredients. She then whipped together a quick salad with mixed greens, cucumbers, and tomatoes after helping Chris make a simple oil and balsamic vinaigrette dressing to toss it all in. After the noodles were cooked and drained, everything was placed on the table.

"Do we have any of that long bread?" Chris asked.

"Yes, we have French bread. That's what the long bread is called. I have some in the refrigerator that I can toast."

"Yum! Can you please?" Chris begged.

Stewart walked in just as Patrice placed the plates on the table.

"Hi babe. Now, look at my domestic goddess. Breakfast *and* dinner, wow. The food smells amazing. How was your day?" Stewart asked as he kissed Grace softly.

"I had a pretty productive day. I think I outdid myself, if I may say so. How did your meeting with the new client go?"

"I think it went well but they wouldn't commit to giving us the account. They apparently want to talk with one more group, but I think we made a solid offer and everyone did a great job with their presentations. Now we just wait."

Dinner conversation was light as Grace didn't want to repeat her encounter with Patrice and she knew the children had homework to complete. After they finished eating and were all clearing the table, Grace helped Patrice and Chris load the dishwasher.

"Catch, Mom," Chris said as he tossed a plastic bowl across the center island to Grace at the sink.

The bowl hit her chest and she noticed that her right breast pained when the bowl hit it. Immediately, her mind went back to the lump.

That night, after making sure everyone was asleep, Grace ran a bubble bath in preparation for a long soak. While in the tub, she did a more thorough breast exam, using a firm, smooth touch with her first two fingers as she made circular motions sequentially around the mass. She then raised her arm and felt under her armpit. She could definitely detect the mass more distinctly this time. She decided to have Dr. Shelley Simpson, a longtime friend since college and now a colleague at the hospital in the oncology division, check it out. She felt a little silly because her recent mammogram had been read as normal. Grace had always been fairly cautious about her health matters after both her parents died from cancer-related illnesses. Her father had pancreatic cancer and her mother had breast cancer.

After going to bed, she tossed and turned before finally falling asleep around midnight. She was awakened by the sound of her alarm clock at 5:30 a.m. Grace rolled over, kissed Stewart, and said, "Rise and shine, sleepyhead."

She then walked into the hallway and yelled, "Guys, it's that time. Get up and get yourselves ready for school."

She could hear Patrice stirring and then growl through a yawn.

"I'm up," Chris yelled back.

Grace went downstairs where she felt she could be alone and called Shelley. She briefly explained the situation and asked if she could be seen as soon as possible for a breast exam.

"Sure, why don't ya come by at three thirty today, if ya 'ave the time?" said Shelley in her native West Indian accent.

"I'll see you then."

Not long after she hung up the phone, Grace heard the side door to the kitchen being unlocked. Alice, Grace's plus-sized, sixty-year-old, African-American housekeeper, walked in.

"Good morning, ma'am! Thanks again for the day off yesterday."

"You're most welcome."

"I came a little early to get the laundry started before I take my babies to school."

"I didn't do much housework yesterday. I did load the dishwasher, though. Mostly, I focused on my Christmas shopping."

"Well, that's good. I'm glad you got some time to yourself."

"Alice, Patrice wanted to talk with you yesterday about something that she didn't want to discuss with me. I know that they see you as a grandmother figure, but I need to know if anything serious is going on with her."

"You know Patrice is at the age where she's noticing boys. I try to keep her talking so that I'll know if anything serious is going on. But, Dr. Livingston, if it was something troubling or something I thought you or Mr. Livingston needed to know, I would certainly tell you."

"I believe you. It's just that she has such a nasty attitude most of the time," said Grace.

"Yes but I think she's just trying to get your attention."

"Oh. Well, thanks Alice. I'd better get myself ready for work and get out of here."

Alice walked away shaking her head as she hung her purse on a hook in the laundry room and started her duties.

"Dr. Livingston needs to slow down and talk with her children. She tries to do way too much," she muttered.

CHAPTER 6

Unlike most days, time seemed to stand still. As 3:25 p.m. rolled around, Grace walked into the oncology clinic's waiting room with its watered-down-coffee colored walls and white baseboards. She spotted the appointment and radiology study check-in signs just beyond several colon cancer prevention displays and breast cancer screening placards throughout the lobby. She went to the check-in window, filled out the prerequisite paperwork, and gave the clerk her insurance card along with her driver's license.

Almost immediately after returning her paperwork to the clerk, she was ushered to the back by a nurse.

"Dr. Simpson told me to come out here to get you and bring you back as soon as possible," said the woman pleasantly.

"I really appreciate you guys working me in today. I hope I'm not disrupting your schedule too much."

"Not at all. Plus, I know you two are good friends. Dr. Simpson sounded like she was really concerned about you."

After being weighed and having her vital signs checked, Grace was taken to an exam room and told to remove her shirt and bra.

"Put on this gown and open it to the front," the nurse requested.

Grace sat on the exam table and looked around the room. As she sat facing a tropical-themed wall mural, she felt less calm and more anxious. Her fingers clung to the thin fabric lining the gown, pulling the two sides together to reduce the cold chill that hung in the air.

After about ten minutes, Shelley, a tall, thin Dominican woman, with long, curly hair and caramel-colored skin, knocked once on the door and then entered the room.

"Hey yuh, what a goin on? You sounded scared dis mawning."

"Oh, I did? I thought I was calm but you know how I am about anything going on with my breasts. Especially with my mom's history and all. I mean, I guess I am nervous."

"I to'tally get it. So, if I heard you right dis mawnin, you think you 'ave a hematoma or somthin' from a fall? When did yuh fall?"

"Ah, a few weeks ago when I was rushing to a department meeting."

"Oh by the way, I heard through the grapevine that yuh got the fellowship directa position. Congratulations!"

"I'm sorry I didn't call you about that. But I haven't had time to let it all sink in. I've just had a lot going on—keeping up with work and the kids.

"Oh, yuh know I undastand. Awright, which breast is it?"

"The right."

Shelley asked Grace to lay back on the exam table. Inspecting both breasts, she then rubbed her hands together to warm them as she asked Grace about the new position. Grace answered distractedly as Shelley's hand moved from the outer portion of her left breast in a slow rocking type of motion from her palm to her fingertips as she systematically moved circularly around her breast. She then moved to the right breast, repeating the same movements. She asked Grace to lift her arms over her head as she examined the right breast more closely.

"I can certainly feel what yuh felt yestaday," Shelley said while continuing to examine Grace's breasts and then palpated her armpit. "So, why don't yuh humor me? Let's repeat yuh mammogram and get a ulta'sound."

Grace thought it was odd but felt better knowing that it wasn't all in her head. Shelley was trying to be thorough. *That's a good thing.* She dressed and headed for the checkout window.

A young woman sitting at the desk said, "I have to get you scheduled for another mammogram and an ultrasound."

"Lucky me," responded Grace.

"Yes ma'am, I'm sorry. Since it's late in the day, I'll have to call in the morning to get these studies scheduled. Is there a particular time that will be good for you?"

"I'll make the time work. Please try to get them scheduled as soon as you can."

"Sure, no problem, Dr. Livingston."

CHAPTER 7

Grace left Shelly's office and headed to the parent-teacher fall conference being held at the kids' school. She and Stewart arrived around the same time. Well's Academy was celebrating its Jubilee Year, signaled by a blue and gold banner hanging over the main entrance. The school was comprised of four buildings, each made of red brick on the bottom half and white stucco on the upper half, with large Corinthian capped columns in front of the main building. They had chosen the school because of its academic achievement record and so their children could go from kindergarten to twelfth grade with the same friends. This especially meant a lot to Stewart because he grew up in a military family and had moved several times during his childhood.

At 5:30 p.m., they each exited their cars and began to walk down a long brick walkway towards the front of the school.

"Hi babe. You have great radar. This is a first for us. I can't remember us ever getting here right on time and at the same time," noted Stewart.

"We're supposed to start at 5:45 p.m. with Chris's teacher first, right?"

"You got it," said Stewart. "You look tired. Is everything okay?"

"I'm fine. It's been a long day. But I do need to talk with you later about a doctor's visit I had with Shelley today."

"With Shelley? What's wrong with her?"

Just as Grace was about to answer, she noticed Mr. Marshall, Chris's teacher, standing inside of the double glass doors at the school's entry, looking down at his watch. He poked his head through the front door and said somewhat impatiently, "You two are the next to the last parents of the day for me. Great timing. Let's get started."

"Hey, it's nice to be great at something I guess," said Stewart, laughing.

"It's nice to see you both," said Mr. Marshall as he walked with them down the corridor past an art exhibit that the elementary school students had created for the school's jubilee celebration.

They eyed colored pencil drawings of buildings that were leaning sideways, covered with stars and American flags, along with columns that looked like birthday candles. Mr. Marshall pointed out Chris's picture of a school building with a flagpole next to it and several small children, or what appeared to be children, standing on the front lawn.

"The kids are so creative," Mr. Marshall commended.

They entered the third door on the right off the hallway. Mr. Marshall turned to Grace and asked her if she remembered that she had agreed to bring cupcakes and punch for the upcoming fall festival on Friday.

"Oh, I sure do. That was at the beginning of the school year that I signed up, wasn't it?" asked Grace.

"Yes, that's right," Mr. Marshall responded.

"I believe I've got it on one of my calendars somewhere. I'll do my best not to forget," said Grace reluctantly.

"Thanks, I know you have a very busy schedule. But I'm sure Chris will remind you as well."

Stewart looked at Grace with a furrowed brow. "Grace, let one of the other moms do that. Or Alice, for Christ's sake. You don't have time."

Grace scowled. "I've got this, okay? I don't want some other mom and even Alice doing for my child what I should be doing. Plus, I agreed to do it so I plan to keep my commitment."

"Okay, superwoman. Whatever."

Grace noticed that Mr. Marshall had looked away with a reddened face while fidgeting with his tie.

Once there was silence in the room, Mr. Marshall cleared his throat.

"Well, let's talk about Chris's progress thus far. As you guys know, he is a good kid. He's bright but can be easily distracted. He's getting most of his work done with frequent redirection but I think he can do better."

He went on to say while laughing, "I think Chris has a future at NASA because I have never seen a kid so fascinated with the stars and planets. I catch him daydreaming a lot and he usually says he's thinking about Mars or Jupiter."

"Based on the grades you sent home so far, I thought he was doing okay. It sounds like you're in disagreement?" Stewart responded.

"And we haven't been told this year about his daydreaming problem," said Grace, shrugging her shoulders.

"No, please don't misunderstand me. Chris is doing well overall. It's just that I think he has the ability to do so much more. I sent a couple of notes home with him, but they were never returned. I assumed you may not have seen them. I planned to discuss this with you all tonight anyway."

"Notes about what?" asked Stewart.

"Basically, I wanted to talk about this very topic. The same things I just mentioned."

He gave them a folder with Chris's progress report and some of his schoolwork. Stewart and Grace looked through the folder together. They saw a few incomplete notes at the tops of pages and grades ranging from As to high Cs.

Stewart turned to Grace. "Do you have any more questions for Mr. Marshall, babe?"

Grace shook her head and got up from her seat. Stewart gave Mr. Marshall a handshake.

"We'll talk with Chris," Stewart said as they left the classroom.

"Hey Grace, do you need to go home? Let me talk with Patrice's teacher. You look like you need to rest."

"No, I need to hear for myself what Ms. McNeely has to say. Patrice challenges me on everything, or at least it feels that way. I want to hear with my own ears if she is doing the same thing at school."

"You're the one who said it's because she's experiencing hormonal changes," Stewart cynically responded.

"I think that's part of it, but—can we talk about this more at home?"

Stewart shrugged. "Do we have to go to the next building for Ms. McNeely's classroom?"

"Yeah, she's in the building on the left," Grace responded absentmindedly, as she stifled a cough.

They were greeted at the door by Ms. McNeely.

"Hi, guys, come on in and take a seat. I'll jump right in because it's getting late and I know we all want to get home. Patrice is quite a precocious young lady. She's always a step ahead of the other children in most of her subjects. She is very respectful and gets along well with all of the other children in her class. I'd like you all to consider having her tested for the gifted program here at the school. I've been told that you decided against it in the past, but I do wish you would reconsider," Ms. McNeely pleaded.

Grace sat in silence as she tried to take in all that had been said. What stood out most to her was the fact that Patrice was very respectful.

Stewart broke the awkward silence by saying, "We appreciate your assessment, but we don't want to put any undue pressure on Patrice. We know that she's a smart girl but she's also at an awkward stage in her life. We don't want to disrupt her routine any more than we have to. Advanced classes can come in high school if she still meets the criteria then. For right now, we just want her to be a kid."

Grace agreed with a nod.

"Well, I have to respect your wishes. But I'm concerned that Patrice tries to intentionally make mistakes on her schoolwork to fit in with her friends. If she was with other high achievers, I believe she would go to a new level in her academics," Ms. McNeely replied. She shared some of Patrice's schoolwork to make her point.

"We'll have a talk with her," Grace responded.

Ms. McNeely hesitated, then she asked Grace, "Are you okay? You look a little drained. Oh, look at me telling the doctor that she doesn't look well."

Grace thanked her for her concern. Then, she and Stewart left the school, got into their respective cars, and headed home.

CHAPTER 8

Alice had warmed up the leftover spaghetti for dinner. "They say they done wit' homework. I ain't much for checking it, but it looked like they were finished," said Alice.

"Thanks, we have to talk about progress reports anyway," said Grace.

Alice peeked over her glasses at the children who had both come into the kitchen when they heard their parents get home. "Y'all bet not be doing bad in school or you gone hafta answer to me."

"I know I've been good," said Chris.

"All right, I'm gone. I'll see y'all tomorrow," said Alice.

After Alice's exit, Grace quickly prepared a fresh salad and asked Patrice to set the table. As Stewart and Grace sat down for dinner with the kids, they talked about their progress reports.

"Patrice, your teacher says you're doing a great job with your schoolwork, but she thinks you may be intentionally trying to get things wrong to fit in with you friends. If that's true, you realize that benefits no one," said Stewart.

Patrice responded hastily, "I know and I'm not intentionally doing my work wrong."

"If your friends don't like that you're a smart girl, maybe they aren't good friends to be around after all," said Stewart.

"Are you interested in that gifted and talented program that we talked with you about last year?" Grace asked. "Daddy and I know that you will do well wherever you are, but we don't want you to miss out on any opportunities that could benefit you."

Patrice made a face. "Mom, most of the kids in those classes hate being in that program. It seems like all they do is complain about their schoolwork. I've looked at some of the books and it doesn't seem that hard to me. But I don't really like the girls in those classes either. If Robin and Arial could go with me, then it might not be so bad."

"Patrice, you can't focus on your friends when you're trying to determine what's best for you academically," Grace cautioned.

"Are you guys going to make me do it this time?"

"No, not at all. We just wanted to hear where you were on that matter. Just promise us that you won't try to hide your intellect. Do your best. Okay?" said Stewart.

Patrice nodded.

Stewart then turned to Christopher and took a deep breath.

"Am I in trouble, Daddy? You look mad."

"Mr. Marshall says you're daydreaming too much and you haven't been getting some of your work done. We weren't aware you'd been warned about this more than once. And apparently, a couple of notes were sent home with you but we never saw them. What's going on, son?"

"It's just that we studied the planets last year and they were my favorite. I like thinking about stuff, like my telescope. Sometimes Mr. Marshall calls on me to answer in class and I try to figure out where they are in the book, but I'm usually wrong. He yelled at me last week and said I needed to get my head out of the clouds. I'm sorry. I'm not trying to be bad at school," Chris said as tears began to roll down his face.

"There's nothing wrong with having a fascination with the planets and stars but you can't let that distract you during school. Surprisingly, your grades aren't too bad, but you're going to fall behind if you keep this up," replied Stewart.

"Yes, sir," said Chris, nodding.

"If you can't focus on schoolwork, you won't get that new telescope you've been asking for," Stewart said sternly.

Grace made a mental note to tell Stewart that she had already bought the telescope.

Stewart and Grace frequently skirted around the need to have Chris tested for ADHD because Grace didn't like the idea of him taking medications but the raised eyebrow and smirk on Stewart's face let Grace know the discussion was far from over.

After the kids were in bed, Grace fell back onto a chaise lounge in their bedroom, positioned in a corner near a set of French doors leading to a small backyard patio.

She groaned, "I'm exhausted."

"Can I talk with you about something that's disturbing me?" asked Stewart.

Grace nodded. "Sure."

"Grace, please hear me out and know that I speak out of love for you. I think you're working too hard and trying to do too much. You don't see yourself. Why didn't you just tell Mr. Marshall to get someone else to bring the stupid cupcakes and punch? That wouldn't have been a big deal. Instead, you just said, okay. And I really am happy that you got the new position you wanted at work, but I see you putting one more thing on an already full plate. Baby, the world is going to keep spinning whether you are here or not."

A tear dropped as Grace said, "I don't know why I push myself so much. I just feel like everybody expects me to be mom and doctor extraordinaire. In all honesty, I feel like you want the *perfect* wife, too! I'm sorry if I've let you down! What I hear when you say that I'm adding *one more thing* to my plate is that I'll have less time to focus on you!"

"Well, forgive me for being selfish! Yes, I do want more time with my wife. Is that so wrong? I'm sure the kids would enjoy more time with their mother!" Stewart exploded.

"I really don't want to go into this again, Stewart! I'm tired and I'm going to sleep!" Grace shouted.

"Why do you do this? Why can't I have a conversation with my wife without you shutting down? We need to have this conversation, Grace. If you want to go to sleep, so be it but weren't you going to talk with me about Shelley or something?" Stewart asked angrily.

"I really don't want to talk about anything else right now if you don't mind," Grace said through a muffled cry. She hurriedly walked into her closet, changed into her pajamas, and got in the bed.

Stewart walked over to the bed. "Are we really doing this again? Grace, can we talk?"

"No, you're right. I'm tired and this discussion would just be one more thing for me to add to my list of issues."

"Issues? I did not say issues. I simply said that you're trying to do too much."

Grace became quiet and forced her eyes closed.

"Okay, I'll let it go and we can do this your way." He got up from the bed and changed into his flannel plaid pajama pants in his closet. After hanging up his clothes, he crawled into bed and turned his back to Grace.

CHAPTER 9

S helley's office staff managed to get Grace scheduled for her mammogram and ultrasound on the following day. Later that day, after Shelley got the results of the test, she called Grace and asked her to come back to the office on Wednesday afternoon. She encouraged her to bring Stewart as well.

"I 'aven't seen Stewart inna while and I would love to si 'im."

"I guess I'll have to get Alice to pick up the kids because it's a practice night and I usually pick them up, but that'll be fine. We don't have to do this all professional and everything. You can just tell me over the phone. You're not trying to get another co-pay out of me are you?" Grace asked in a humorous but frightened tone.

"Of course not, you are mi patient and you will get treated like any otha patient, my dear."

Later that evening, Grace sat down in the family room in an oversized nubuck brown leather chair across from Stewart who was lounging on the beige sectional sofa, reading through some work papers. His head was bowed as he looked through his bifocals. When Grace told him that she needed to talk with him, he placed the papers on a small end table near the sofa.

"Shoot, what's going on? But before you get started, I'm sorry about how things went down the other night," Stewart said.

"I'm sorry, too. But that's not what I want to talk about," Grace responded and muffled a cough. "Do you remember the fall I had at work?"

"Of course I do. Has your knee healed up?"

"Yes, my knee is fine. But I thought I also told you that I hit my chest on the steps, right?"

Stewart nodded.

"Well, after that incident, I thought I felt a lump in my breast. It was sore and I decided to see Shelley just to be sure it was okay. She asked me to get a mammogram and an ultrasound. Now she wants us both to come in on Wednesday to talk about it," Grace spouted.

"Wait, didn't you have a mammogram like three months ago or something? I remember you telling me it was normal."

"I did but she asked me to repeat it."

"So, why do I need to be there to talk about your mammogram? Is that all she said?" Stewart asked puzzled.

"No, she said she hadn't seen you in a while. Other than that, I don't know why she wants you to be there. I'm just praying it's nothing bad."

"Oh, that wouldn't even make sense. They told you that last mammogram was normal, right? Things don't change that fast do they?"

"That's true."

"Of course I'll be there and I'll let Shelley know she doesn't have to resort to extreme measures to see me," laughed Stewart.

They arrived at Shelley's office at 4:25 p.m. on Wednesday afternoon and the same nurse who had taken Grace to the exam room a few days prior met them at a different door and led them to the back hallway where Shelley's personal office was located. The nurse seated them in two mahogany finished box arm guest chairs in front of Shelley's cherry wood L-shaped desk.

Initially, Stewart and Grace sat in silence. Grace tried to deflect from the disquieting hush by saying softly, "Shelley's family pictures are nice, aren't they?"

"Yes they are," said Stewart.

Shelley entered the room with a quick knock on the door.

"Hi, guys, sorry for di wait. I just finished with mi las' patient for di day. Well, technically yuh di las' patient, Grace, but yuh kno wah I mean."

Her West Indian accent was always more pronounced when she was with friends.

Both Grace and Stewart stood to give Shelley a hug.

"Can I get yuh all somethin' to drink?" She walked over to a small refrigerator that was stored on the farthest side of the bookcase behind her desk.

"No thanks," they both said in unison as they sat back down.

Shelley took a bottle of Perrier from the refrigerator and twisted off the top. The fizzing sound filled the air as they both followed her movement around the room. Shelley asked about the kids and how Stewart's company was coming along.

"Everything is going well. How have you and your family been?" Stewart asked.

"Michelle is already a freshman at Duke. Time moves so quickly. Miguel is inna eigh' grade at St. Aloysius. He's playing football an givin' his mama a heart attack wid each game. Mi husband thinks I'm too protective."

"I know Grace gets to see you from time to time here at the hospital but I think it's been almost six months since I actually laid eyes on you."

"I know, right? We're all jus' too busy these days."

"You look great and it looks like life has been treating you kindly. We must do better. Grace and I will have to have you guys over for dinner."

"Dat's a deal."

"As for the company, all is well," said Stewart. Then he looked over at Grace. "Can you fit Shelley into that schedule of yours for dinner? My wife is a busy beaver who can't say no to people or this hospital. One can only hope she can find time for an old friend."

"Okay, enough of the sarcasm," said Grace.

"So, Shelley, my wife needs you to take away her fears. I told her that this was not going to be anything more than a social visit."

Shelley walked over from the bookcase and sat in her chair. She looked at Grace directly. "Okay, here's the issue. The mammogram *is* abnormal and the ultrasound confirmed it. The radiologist described it as a 2.5 cm irregular spiculated lesion in the right upper outer quadrant of your right breast. That correlates wid what wi both felt."

"What? Wait a minute. Do you think this is cancer?" Grace asked as she put her hand to her chest.

"Grace, these findings are highly suspicious of cancer but we need to 'ave a biopsy done before we move any furtha," Shelley warned.

Stewart tried to speak but his words exited as a whisper.

"Shelley, wait. I thought Grace was told her mammogram was fine no more than three months ago."

Shelley moved her gaze from Grace to Stewart.

"You're absolutely right. I had three of our radiologists go over the films again and again and they said that it was not apparent on the previous mammogram. I really don't kno 'ow to explain it, Stewart. I'll get Grace scheduled for a biopsy tomorrow mawnin, if you would like to do it then."

Grace sat motionless.

"Get it scheduled as soon as you can."

CHAPTER 10

Still healing from the breast biopsy, Grace and Stewart found themselves back in Shelley's office sitting in the same armchairs. Only this time, they were holding hands. Shelley was already seated at her desk when they arrived.

"Okay, I know yah wan' the results," Shelley said in a somber tone. She took a deep breath. "I'm so sorry but the biopsy was positive fir a high-grade cancer, poorly differentiated invasive lobular adenocarcinoma, HER 2 negative."

"What?" Grace exclaimed. "You have got to be joking! *Poorly differentiated?* This makes no sense. How long has this been in me?" She closed her hands over her mouth and began to cry.

Stewart frowned, got up from his chair, looked out the window, and asked as he looked back over his shoulder at Shelley, "Lobular adenocarcinoma? What does that mean?"

"In layman's terms Stewart, she 'ave what appears to be a' advanced cancer. Grace, unfortunately, lobular carcinoma is more easily missed on mammograms than ductal cancers. I don't like that the pathologist called it poorly differentiated, also. We 'ave got to work out a treatment plan for you."

She got up from her desk and stood beside Grace with her hand on her friend's shoulder.

Stewart continued to look blurry-eyed out of the window.

"Are you telling me that my wife is dying?"

"No, I'm not sa'in that she is dyin' but we will 'ave an uphill battle with this. Grace, I'm goin' to 'ave to schedule you for a full body PET/CT scan since you have had that cough and shortness of breath. I'll try to get these tests done as soon as possible. I'll also get you an appointment with Dr. Huggins who is the best breast surgeon in town."

Grace nodded but didn't really absorb what was being said. She sat motionless, feeling like all the air in the room had vanished and she was desperately trying to catch her breath. Finally, when she could speak again, she said, "You know, I think I was trying to prepare myself for cancer but not *poorly differentiated*. This is crazy. How long has this been there and what am I looking at here?"

Stewart came back over, sat down next to Grace, and grabbed her hand.

"We will do anything and everything we need to do to beat this. So, we meet this surgeon and get X-rays, then what? Do we need to go to MD Anderson in Houston? I've always heard that they're the best for cancer treatment, right?"

"Well, I think she's in good 'ands 'ere. We follow MD Anderson protocols."

"So, again, we meet the surgeon and get a PET scan, then what?" Stewart asked Shelley.

"Well, once she 'ave surgery and the X-rays, then I can better tell yuh about our chemotherapy plan an whether we need to consider radiation as well."

Grace nodded as Shelley gave Stewart some pamphlets about breast cancer and explained what Grace could expect and what Stewart should do to support Grace throughout the treatment.

Grace stared at a rectangular decorative glass ceramic floor tile in front of Shelley's desk with the University of Tennessee logo embedded in it and felt a deep awareness of her parents suffering through their cancer illnesses. She remembered the hair loss, nausea, vomiting, and diarrhea. *It's happening again.* She felt as though she needed to push a heavy weighted dome off of her head. She began to cough and felt as though she was choking. Shelley offered her a bottle of water.

"No thanks," said Grace, pushing it away. "Um, I can't listen to this anymore. I want to go home and try to let all of this sink in. I'm sorry, Shelley."

"I undastand, Grace. This is a lot of information to take in at once. I'll call to check on yuh later. If yuh 'ave any questions, please don't 'esitate to ask."

They each hugged Shelley and said goodbye as they exited through a side door that led to the parking lot. Stewart opened the front passenger's door for Grace as she settled into her seat and buckled her seatbelt. He drove home while Grace sat in silence.

Grace's jaw flinched as she felt a numbing sadness overtaking her. She turned suddenly toward Stewart and cried, "What have I done to deserve this? I have been a good person all my life. I wasn't a troublemaking kid or a wild child that tried to make other people's lives miserable. I mean, what good did it do me to exercise every day, take all those stupid vitamins, and eat whole grains with *every* meal! Cancer still found me!"

Tears covered her eyes but she made no movement to brush them away.

A line in Stewart's jaw twitched as he gripped the steering wheel and drove ahead.

Lowering her voice, she said, "I've sat patients down for years to tell them they have various forms of cancers and thought I showed compassion. But in all honesty, I never really felt the true weight of their pain. Well, I guess it's my time and this hurts like hell."

Tears began to roll down her cheeks.

"Babe, hang in there. You are a terrific person. Nobody deserves cancer. This is definitely not what I expected, either. Even when Shelley told us that the mammogram was abnormal, I think I hoped it all was a mistake. Maybe even more than you did."

"What do you mean more than me? Do you think I *want* to have cancer?"

"Of course not. I just mean that I'm confused and sad, too. I hope you know that I'm not trying to say anything to upset you any more than you already are."

Grace sat quietly looking out the passenger window and nodded.

"What will I do about that new position at work and the kids...and their school? Friday is the day of the fall festival party for Chris's class. I really don't want to go but I promised."

"Stop it! There you go again. You're worrying about everybody else! You need to focus on your own survival right now! I'm sorry, but enough is enough! You are as human as the next person—let go of the Mother Teresa act. I need you to be here—I need you!" yelled Stewart as he rapped his fist against the steering wheel.

Grace became quiet again.

CHAPTER 11

When they arrived home, Stewart walked Grace to their bedroom.

"You need to try to get some rest. I'll call Mr. Marshall and let him know that I'll have Alice drop off punch and cupcakes or whatever can be found on Friday morning. You don't need to go to that school."

"I can't fight you on that." She undressed and put on pink and blue satin pajamas. "Can you please have the kids come in and say goodnight since I'm going to bed so early?"

"Sure," he said, leaving the room. Then he poked his head back in. "By the way, I'm sorry I exploded in the car."

"We both need some rest," said Grace.

Patrice was the first to enter the room. "Mom, are you feeling okay? Dad said you had a really rough day," said Patrice with a compassionate stare.

"I'm fine. Just a lousy day."

"Is there anything I can do to help you?"

"No baby, but I do appreciate your concern," Grace said as she brushed back Patrice's hair.

They heard the doorbell ring as Patrice gave Grace a hug.

Chris jumped on the bed.

"Hey Mom, Daddy said you won't be able to go to the fall festival on Friday. He told me not to ask too many questions but why can't you go?"

"Some things have come up that I have to take care of. I just overbooked myself, buddy. I'm sorry."

"Okay, but you're going to miss the sweets. Plus, we're going to have an inflatable slide."

"Well, you have my permission to eat my portion of the goodies and go down the slide at least once for me. Deal?"

"Deal," responded Chris as they gave each other a high five.

Stewart walked in from the kitchen carrying a steaming cup of chamomile tea.

"All right, that's enough. I told you guys to just do a short stay because Mom needs some rest." He placed the cup on a tumbled marble stone coaster on the bedside table near Grace.

"Thanks, sweetheart," Grace said as she looked up with a warm smile and hugged Patrice and Chris again.

"Aw, do we have to go already?" asked Chris.

"Already," Stewart stated, as he placed his hands on each of their shoulders and walked them to the bedroom door. "Dinner is on the table. I ordered burgers."

"Yes!" said Chris.

Patrice looked back at Grace. "Goodnight, mom. I love you."

"I love you back," said Grace.

"You guys need to eat, get your baths, finish your homework, and get in bed once you've finished with everything," said Stewart.

Grace propped herself up on two pillows, sitting almost upright, and reached for her tea. Stewart walked over after closing the door and began rubbing her back as he stood beside her.

"How are you feeling?"

"I'm okay I guess. Did you notice how Patrice was acting? She knows there is more to me being in bed than just being overworked."

"She's a sensitive child and even though you guys are sometimes like oil and water, she loves and cares about you," said Stewart. "I think we should get as much information as we can before we tell them. What do you think?"

"I agree. I'm not sure I can tell them anything without breaking down, anyway. This is all surreal. In a matter of a few weeks, I have fallen down a flight of stairs, both literally and figuratively, headlong into a place where I hoped I would never be. And unfortunately, I haven't a clue of where I'll land. My brain feels like mush. I've got no answers right now."

"I certainly understand. I don't have any medical knowledge but this seems to have happened too fast for me, as well."

"I have so many things I'll need to think through. I mean, the added burdens on you with the kids and then the burden I'm putting on everyone at work. Plus, the holidays are just around the corner. I guess I'll have to talk with Dr. Malloy tomorrow about changing my work schedule. This couldn't have happened at a worse time."

Stewart walked over to his closet and started to change his clothes. "I'm listening to you—just want to get comfortable."

"Okay."

"Look, you don't have try to figure everything out tonight; you need to get some rest," Stewart encouraged through a muffled voice.

"It's just that I know what the surgery is usually like for people," Grace said, blinking back tears, "especially having gone through breast cancer with Mama. I have a good idea of the type of chemotherapy they'll use, even though Shelley said she'd have to figure that out after my surgery. Most of that stuff makes people feel horrible. Plus, I just pray the surgery goes well. I've seen people develop lymphedema from the lymph node dissection."

"Grace, don't do this to yourself. Don't expect the worst scenarios to happen. What is lymphedema, anyway?"

"Do you remember when Shelley said I would need lymph nodes under my arm removed to make sure there is no cancer there? Well, that part of the surgery can result in permanent swelling of the arm. Sometimes, it can be debilitating. I've seen women who've had to wear a compression sleeve on their arm because the swelling was so bad," Grace said anxiously. "Then there is the possibility of getting neuropathy in my fingers from the chemotherapy which is equally as bad."

"Neuropathy?" asked Stewart with hunched shoulders.

"Oh, I'm sorry, numbness in the fingers or toes."

"Hmmm."

"Either one of those complications could mean that I wouldn't be able to do procedures in the future. It happened to one of the general surgeons a few years back and she had to leave her practice...," said Grace, her voice trailing off.

Stewart reentered the room wearing a pair of flannel pajama pants and a t-shirt. He positioned himself midway in the bed and laid his head on Grace's lap.

She took a big gulp of tea, looked into his eyes, and said, "I don't know why, but I feel I need to go home before I go through this. You never know how this kind of thing can go."

Stewart lifted his brow. "Home? What do you mean? Are you referring to Mississippi because this is your home, baby."

"Yes, I mean Mississippi. I know you moved around a lot as a kid, but Mississippi is my birthplace. It's where I spent my entire childhood. Of course this is my home with you and the kids, but Mississippi is my home, too."

He nodded. "I get it. I mean, it's your decision and I'm certainly okay with what you feel you need to do. But, maybe I didn't completely understand Shelley. I think everything is going to be okay once you have the surgery. We have to keep a positive outlook."

Grace smiled timidly, looked away from Stewart, and focused on the pamphlets Shelley had given them, now lying on the dresser.

Stewart propped himself on his left elbow, reached up and wiped away a tear from Grace's eye. "I think going home to Mississippi will be good for you. Why don't we go there this Friday? We can leave after the kids get out of school."

"Actually, I think I'd like to go by myself. I think the time away will give me space to think about everything rolling around in my head. What do you think about that?"

"Look, I'm okay with whatever you think you need right now. But do you think you're strong enough to make the trip by yourself?"

"I think I am. I know I've been tired but I'll pace myself. I'll call Hanna and let her know I'm coming and I'll ask her to let the others know that I'm planning a visit. I don't want to have too many other conversations until I get there."

Stewart rested his head back on Grace's lap and closed his eyes. Grace looked down at him and rubbed his head.

"If I haven't said it today, I love you baby," she said.

"Love you, too," Stewart mumbled groggily.

Grace sat and stared at Stewart for a few more minutes as he snored. She nudged him gently and asked him to get under the covers on his side of the bed. She leaned over and kissed his forehead, hoping that she too could fall asleep. But as she listened to his monotonous whiffs and whistles, she smiled with tears falling as she realized how melodious his sleep noises sounded to her now. She promised herself that she wouldn't complain about it anymore as she laid her head on his chest and savored being able to hear his muffled heartbeat through the flapping growls.

CHAPTER 12

Early the following morning, Grace picked up her cell phone and called Dr. Hank Malloy. Hydraulic whirling noises filled the background.

"Hank, thanks for answering."

"You never call my cellphone, so I was concerned there was an emergency or something at the hospital."

"No, I'm sorry. Did I startle you? You sound like you're out of breath."

"Nope, I'm on the bicycle at the campus gym right now."

"Okay, again, sorry for the interruption. But I really need to see you first thing this morning because I need to discuss some things with you that are fairly important."

"All right, I'll finish up my workout now. I can meet you in about thirty-five minutes at my office. Will that give you enough time?"

"Plenty," said Grace as she thanked him and ended the call.

She had been up since three that morning and was dressed by five. She had peeked her head into the children's rooms a few times before waking them at five forty-five to get ready for their day.

"I've got to go to the hospital earlier than usual. Fix you a bowl of cereal for breakfast and Alice will get you to school. Daddy knows I'm headed out," Grace explained as she entered each of their rooms.

"Are you feeling better, mom?" asked Patrice.

"I'm fine, baby. Like I said, I have to be at work extra early today. I want you to work hard today at school and make mama proud."

"Yes ma'am," responded Patrice.

At 6:25 a.m., she parked in the physician's parking lot nearest the gastroenterology department building and sat listening to the radio. Twenty minutes later, she exited the car wearing a blue scrub suit and a white lab coat and headed for Dr. Malloy's office. After walking through a large white wooden door, she saw him standing in the foyer with slicked back wet hair.

"Good morning Grace," he bellowed.

"Hey Hank, thanks again for interrupting your workout for me," she responded softly.

"You sounded like you were anxious on the phone. Let's walk back to my office and talk."

"Sure," Grace replied as she followed him down the hall to the largest office off the corridor.

He offered her a seat. "Okay, so what's up?"

She went through all that had happened during the past few weeks and how she was given her diagnosis the day prior.

She then focused on a diagram of a liver hanging on the wall behind his head and began to ramble.

"So you see, I'll need some time off. If it's not a problem, I need to start that time tomorrow. I have a lot of tests to do and have to meet with the surgeon next week. I can work abbreviated days if you need me during that time. Shelley has me tentatively scheduled for surgery in a week or so. Things are moving fast right now. I know the timing couldn't be worse. I plan to try to return to work as soon as I can. I'm guessing I'll be out for about three to four weeks. I've decided I'll probably schedule my chemotherapy on Fridays so that I won't have to miss much work during that time. I know this puts you in a tough place with the department."

Dr. Malloy sat quietly as Grace fidgeted in her chair. His eyes narrowed and his forehead appeared to pulsate in Grace's mind as he said, "I'm so sorry to hear that you have cancer, Grace. Of course, I will make adjustments in your schedule. You need to focus on getting well. As for your concerns about work, please, don't worry. I'll fill in until you get back."

"I just hate that you'll have to alter your schedule for me."

"Oh, please, I'll be fine. The fellows won't be happy when they realize it's me and not you teaching them." He forced a smile.

"I doubt that."

"Listen, I want you to be kind to yourself and don't try to do too much. You are a valuable asset to this department and we need you back as healthy as you can be."

"That's certainly a kind thing to say."

"Why don't you go back home? We'll figure out how to manage your schedule for today, as well."

Grace couldn't hold back her tears. "Thank you so much. This has knocked me off my feet. I hate being a burden on everyone."

Hank got up from his desk and gently placed his hand on her shoulder.

"Grace, things happen to all of us that are out of our control. You'll get through this. But as for us here at this place, don't worry at all. We'll be right here when you get back."

Grace got up from her chair.

"Please let us know if you need anything. I'll call Stewart and check on you guys from time to time, if that's okay?"

"Thanks, that'll be fine," said Grace, looking back over her shoulder.

She turned around and hugged Dr. Malloy briefly before leaving his office. She looked up at the poster-sized faculty photo of all of her colleagues in the department as she walked down the hallway and continued to cry softly. After leaving the building, she walked along the shrubbery lined stone path to the parking lot and got back into her car.

She started the engine and was about to shift the car into gear when she began to scream, "No! No! No!" followed by a deep guttural moan.

She then shouted, "Lord, why are you letting this happen?!"

Grace cried for several more minutes and began to cough uncontrollably. She pulled a cough drop out of her pocket, unwrapped it with shaky hands, and popped it into her mouth. She grabbed a bottle of water that she kept in her glove compartment and took several gulps. Patting her eyes dry, she decided to call her sister Hanna.

CHAPTER 13

Hanna picked up on the second ring.

"Hanna? It's Grace," Grace called out over her car phone speaker in a nasally voice.

"I know who you are. I have caller ID," Hanna said, amused.

"I'm coming home tomorrow for a few days. I have something important to share with you guys."

"Do you have a cold? You sound congested."

"No, no, I don't," Grace said quickly.

"Well, whatcha sharing now? Another dog-gone promotion? Give us little folk a break, Grace," she said, laughing.

Grace sighed, sucked in a big gulp of air, and cried, "Um, I didn't want to tell you this over the phone...but I'm gonna need you to be a strong shoulder for me when I get there."

"Okay, wait, now you're scaring me. What's going on?"

"I—I was, um, told I have breast cancer. Uh, I'm, um—" Grace cried.

After her statement, there was no communication aside from the deep sounds of respirations on Hanna's end and crying on Grace's. After a few seconds, she heard Hanna say, "Calm down, Grace. You know I'm here for you."

Grace tried to cut off her cry but groaned, "Lord have mercy! Lord have mercy! Lord have mercy!"

"Grace, where are you right now? Is Stewart there?"

"No, I'm in the parking lot at work."

"At work? Why are you at work? Do I need to call Stewart to come and get you?"

"No, I'm fine. I'm headed back home. I just finished talking with my boss," she said through sniffles. "I promise you that I didn't plan to have a meltdown on you. It's just that after talking with Dr. Malloy, your voice was what I needed to hear."

"Honestly, in a million years, I wouldn't have guessed that you would've been calling about this. Okay, so, wow, what time will you guys arrive tomorrow?"

"Oh, I'm coming by myself. Stewart and the kids aren't coming with me because I wanted some alone time," Grace responded, still sniffling.

"What? Are you sure you don't need me to come up there and ride back here with you? You know I have frequent flyer miles that I can put to use."

"No, I'll be fine. Can you just hold me up when I get there, though?"

"Of course. How bad is it? What kind of prognosis did your doctor give you?"

"I promise I'll fill you in on all of that when I get there. I just can't talk about it right now." Grace pulled a tissue out of her purse and wiped her eyes. "Can you just let everyone else know I'll be in Jackson tomorrow? But Hanna, I want to tell them about this myself."

"Sure, no problem. You're gonna stay with me, okay?"

"That'll be great. I hope the others won't be offended that I didn't call them, too. But I'm a wreck right now."

"They'll be fine. I'll handle things on this end," urged Hanna. "Hey Grace, you know I always put my money on you whenever there's a fight, right?"

Grace grinned. "Thanks, Hanna. I'll see you tomorrow. I love you," she said softly.

"Love you back. See you soon."

Grace sat for a few more minutes before starting the engine and slowly rolling out of the parking lot. As she passed the big orange University of Tennessee Hospital sign, she thought about Hanna calling her a fighter. This would be the ultimate fight for her life indeed.

But as she reflected on Hanna's statement about her fighter nature, she thought of the incident that bonded her and Hanna as teens. Her mind drifted to her tenth-grade year in high school when Kenneth Jones, the star of the track team, tried to rape her. She recalled how she thought her brother didn't like him because he was a faster runner and had a braggadocios air that Samuel felt an underclassman shouldn't have. She later found out that Samuel knew more about Kenneth's character, giving him greater distaste for his fellow track mate. Grace recalled confiding in Hanna that Kenneth had asked her out on a date and that she was planning to go. She knew she would have to lie to their parents because they would have said no. A made-up story about doing a project with a friend was her ruse for getting out of the house. Hanna didn't like it but promised to keep her secret. She remembered that their date started with a secret pick up spot at the neighborhood park, followed by the much-anticipated movie, *Die Hard*, at The Alamo Theatre where Grace and Kenneth held hands.

After leaving the movie, they stopped by Kenneth's house to pick up a box of candy which he said he had intended to bring with him. He invited her into the dark house. Kenneth pretended to trip on something in the foyer. While Grace looked for the light switch, he reached out his hand, asking for help. When she reached down to help him up, he pulled her hard to the floor and started kissing her forcibly. He pinned her to the floor and pressed himself against her. She relived her attempt to scream as he placed his hand over her mouth, tore her blouse, and tried to reach for her breasts. She lifted her knee into his crotch with as much strength as she could muster. She vividly remembered his screams as he fell into the floor and she ran out of the front door, almost knocking Samuel over as she exited. Evidently, Hanna had made Samuel aware of the tryst, despite her promise of confidentiality. Grace recalled her relief in seeing Samuel run into the house. He checked to see that she was okay and then punched Kenneth repeatedly until Kenneth threw up.

She, Hanna, and Samuel kept her secret and the way that Hanna consoled her after she returned home created a lasting bond between the two of them.

"Fighters," Grace said softly as she drove home.

CHAPTER 14

O n Friday at 4:30 a.m., Grace awakened to the sound of a familiar gospel tune, *Healing*, coming from the wireless tabletop speakers nestled on the edge of their dresser. Stewart walked out of the bathroom singing along with the music.

"I beat you getting up this morning. So, I can say rise and shine to you, sleepyhead—for a change," he said with a wide grin. "I've got coffee brewing and muffins warming in the oven."

"Why are you so upbeat?" yawned Grace.

"Because I'm hopeful that God will give you the peace you need about surgery, chemotherapy, and whatever else this disease might bring our way. We're going to beat this."

Grace shrugged. "I hope so. You know, I need this trip. I need to see my family. I want to go by my parents' old house, too."

"I want you on the road as early as possible. So, up and at 'em."

She scrunched her nose. "It sounds like you're trying to get rid of me."

"That is the last thing I would ever do," replied Stewart as he walked over and kissed her pouting lips. "Get your shower, superwoman."

Grace stretched again and settled her feet on the floor. She searched around for her slippers with her feet using her toes as a guide. She then lazily trudged to the bathroom, took a double look in the mirror, and noticed the dark circles around her eyes. She couldn't decide if she was imagining that she looked sick or if she really did look awful.

She took a quick shower, sat at her vanity, rubbed face cream over her entire face in an upward motion, put concealer under her lower eyelids, applied a peachy-pink blush to her cheeks, and rolled muted berry-colored lipstick on her lips. She then put on a pair of jeans and a purple t-shirt along with a denim jacket. After packing the last of her toiletries in a leather duffel, she pulled on a pair of brown leather boots and headed towards the kitchen. She picked up her cell phone and realized she had missed a text message from Hanna.

> Excited about your stay. Everyone's stopping by the house late tomorrow. Not sure when you want to talk with them, though. Drive carefully.

Grace thought for a second before she replied.

> Sorry I missed your text last night. We can talk when I get there. See you soon. Love you.

Lemon poppy seed muffins sat in the middle of the kitchen table. She grabbed one and took a bite. It was soft, warm, and melted in her mouth. She picked up her thermos and filled it close to the brim watching the rise of steam above the dark liquid.

"I think I'll drink my coffee black today," she said and looked over at Stewart who was leaning against the counter near the refrigerator. "Hanna texted me last night but I just saw the message a few minutes ago. She's asking if I'm going to let everyone know later today when they come by her house. What do you think?"

"Babe, it's up to you. You know your family better than I do. But are you asking because you're concerned about her suggestion?"

"I don't know. Should I just spit it out when I get there or wait until tomorrow?"

"I'm not sure. But didn't you mention something about going by your parents' place at some point? What about asking everyone to meet you there since you always seem to be happy and get good energy there."

"Good idea. I'll think about it. I may just go with the flow of the day and see where that takes me."

"Whatever works for you, babe."

"Shouldn't I wake up the kids?"

"No, you said enough last night, and you definitely kissed them enough."

Grace then began to reel, "By the way, I haven't had a chance to tell Alice thank you for coming to my rescue for the fall festival today. Remind me to call her, okay? Also, remember that Patrice has gymnastics practice tomorrow and Chris has soccer practice. I laid out clothes for Chris for church on Sunday. Sometimes, he can come up with crazy outfits. And—"

"Grace, like you say to me, *I've got this.* You only need to take care of you right now. The kids won't break into pieces because you've left them alone with me. Patrice and Chris are quite capable of telling me where they're supposed to be and when. I'll tell Alice thanks this morning and that's good enough."

"Remember, I don't want Alice to know anything yet, especially before we tell the kids. This is difficult for me. I'm usually the one organizing everything. I feel like I'm letting them down."

"Grace, you have to let go of the reins. Stop trying to manage everything and everybody. This diagnosis has caught us both off guard and while you want everything planned out and known, that's not our reality. I get it." He walked over and hugged her. "We'll be okay. I played that gospel song to encourage you this morning."

"I admire your faith. In all honesty, my faith is pretty weak right now."

"I understand. Fortunately, I have enough for both of us."

After sharing a kiss, Grace followed as Stewart loaded her bags into the back of the SUV. They embraced once again before he opened the driver's side door and Graced settled inside. She started the engine and saw smoke billowing in the rearview mirror as she took a few seconds to let the car warm up.

Stewart went and stood in the doorway. She shifted the gear into reverse and backed out of the driveway, partly looking in the rearview mirror but mostly looking forward and waving at Stewart, who was now standing in the garage with his coffee cup and smiling and waving goodbye.

CHAPTER 15

Grace began her journey home to Mississippi via I-75 south towards Chattanooga. She turned her radio dial from her usual smooth jazz station to 94.9 FM, Praise Radio. Though she rarely listened to gospel music, she liked the inspiration she felt when Stewart played the gospel song earlier. But instead of music, she heard a talk show host ask, "Do you think angels are real? Do you think they protect us in times of need and if so, how? Well, that's our topic for this morning. I hope you can join the discussion."

Grace quickly turned down the volume and considered his questions. *Of course angels are real. Why would he even have a topic like that?*

She turned the volume back up and listened to the first caller belligerently insist that people took the Bible too literally. Angels weren't flying around with wings, hovering over people like sympathetic harpies. No, they weren't even real.

Grace shook her head and decided that she didn't feel like entertaining such negativity about spiritual things or any other issues this morning. She said aloud, "God, if you're out there, I'm pretty sure I at least still believe in you. I think I do at least believe in angels if that gives me any brownie points in this whole cancer thing."

While Stewart still seemed to be so sure of his faith, Grace considered how hers had waned over the years. She couldn't pinpoint when it happened but accepted that little by little, it had decreased. She thought about how as her job moved more and more to the forefront of her life, church attendance lost its value. She moved from monthly to sporadic Sunday worship services. Sunday had become her day to catch up on things she needed to do at the house or sleep in late.

She hoped Stewart had salvaged their kids by taking them to Sunday school off and on which he believed was important for them. She felt a wave of comfort overcome her as she heard Stewart's voice saying, *We have to rest in the trust that we say we have in God.* She turned the dial to soft jazz and smiled as a familiar melody filled the car.

The sky was black and littered with stars. Crisp, cool air seeped in, ignoring the weatherstrip encasing her window. As she was swept into the fall breeze, she marveled at the contrast in temperature from only a few days before.

As she drove, the sky morphed from black to gray to blue with bright orange hues in what felt like a brief minute. The scene was mesmerizing. Grace had mapped out her travel and figured she would be in Chattanooga by 5:30 a.m. and in Birmingham around eight, just in time for rush hour, unfortunately.

As she passed a sign for Noccalula Falls in Gadsden, Alabama, she recalled how much fun she and the children had during the few times they had stopped there on their trips to Mississippi as a family. The kids loved the Falls' petting zoo and the ninety-foot waterfall. She hoped there would many more trips there in the future.

Attempting to avoid sadness, she turned the music up and lost herself in the sounds. In Birmingham, on I-20 West, she found the morning traffic to be moving at a faster pace than she had anticipated.

At 11:00 a.m., Grace turned onto Tracewoods Drive in her hometown of Jackson, Mississippi. In spite of the long journey, she immediately smiled. As she admired the familiar American Elm tree-lined street, fond memories dropped into her spirit. She softly spoke the words of the Joyce Kilmer poem, "Trees," as she hugged the curves on the winding road.

She remembered having to memorize that poem her eleventh-grade English class. Her teacher had required the class to learn a poem that expressed what they felt was special about where they lived and why.

She slowed down and looked around. She drove up the sloped driveway of her parents' red brick home and parked in the garage, spotting an overwhelming number of spider webs on the walls and ceiling. She also noticed the two rusted garbage cans sitting in the same corner that they had occupied since her childhood. Still gripping the steering wheel, she sat in the car for a while before deciding to call Stewart.

"Hi, Babe, did you just get there? How was the drive?"

"Yeah, I'm here. I'm sitting in the garage at my parents' place now but I haven't gone inside yet."

"Are you feeling okay?"

"Oh, I'm fine and the drive was fine. I didn't really stop except to fill up the car in Tuscaloosa and at Mr. Ishi's Diner once I got here. Luckily, they were still serving breakfast."

"Okay, so what's going on? Why are you still outside?"

"I don't know. It's just that this is so hard. I wish I could run in the house and yell for Mama and Daddy and say that I'm home. Am I making sense?"

"Babe, I understand. Take your time and relax if you can," pleaded Stewart.

"I'll do my best. How are the kids? Was Chris able to get ready for school without too much fuss? And Lord, was Patrice okay?"

"Let's see, the kids are fine, and yes, Chris was a bit hyper, but we managed. You would be so proud of Patrice. She's been a jewel. She actually asked a lot of questions about how you were feeling before you left." Grace took a deep breath.

"You just made me smile. Hug them for me and tell Patrice that I'm proud of her."

"Will do."

"I guess I had better go inside. I'll call you when I get to Hanna's later today."

"Why don't you just call me before you go to bed? I want you to enjoy time with your family."

"I'll do that," Grace replied before saying goodbye.

CHAPTER 16

Grace opened the door to her past as she turned the key in the deadbolt, trying to balance the plastic bag holding her breakfast. Eyeing familiar, dingy white curtains framed by faint rays of the sun's light, she felt welcomed by the house. Those old curtain had hung over the kitchen sink for years. She pulled the cord gently as the screws holding the rod in place began partially releasing themselves from the wall. A brightness glowed over the kitchen overtaking the darkness of the room once the curtains were fully parted.

Grace inhaled and looked around, noticing that the kitchen was fairly tidy. Perhaps one of her siblings had been by to do some cleaning recently. She smiled as she rubbed her hands over the gold-toned laminate countertop. She tossed her purse on the counter and walked into the almost empty den.

Brushing off a space first, she sat down on a lone faded plaid sofa. It was dusty and a little damp. She looked around the room and her memories reawakened. She envisioned the Vincent van Gogh print of a sailboat hanging above the fireplace and then imagined her dad's recliner positioned under the large window next to that fireplace, at just the right angle for the best view of the wide screen floor console television. She craned her neck and eyed the faded silhouettes of where a collage of family photos used to hang above the sofa where she sat. Her parent's wedding picture once hung in the center surrounded by pictures of her and her siblings, Sara, Hanna, Naomi, and Samuel, as babies wearing the same christening gown handed down over the years.

Grace took off her denim jacket, kicked off her cowboy boots, and sank her sock-covered feet into the frayed carpet as she had done so many times before. She was spent and at a loss for how this would all play out. She felt overwhelmed by her health issues. Not to mention, not knowing how her siblings and children would react to her diagnosis. She couldn't take any more teary-eyed looks of pity. She hoped the next couple of days would be a time of clarity and reflection. Although her distraction about leaving Stewart with the kids shaded her thoughts, she tried to soothe her conscience with the fact that Stewart thought this visit would be good for her, too.

She hoped that being back in her childhood home would calm some of her fears. The old red brick house had always been a place where she felt love and affirmation. When she was younger, she thought she could speak and hear clearly from God there. Maybe just being around the house could help spark a born-again experience. Maybe, maybe not, she thought skeptically.

Grace pulled her breakfast out of the bag and ate a few bites of a fried egg sandwich, nibbled on her hash browns, and chased it down with a few sips of orange juice. She had noticed that her taste for food had begun to decrease, possibly a result of the progression of her cancer or depression—maybe both. But, being a country girl at heart, she hoped her appetite would be rehabilitated being around all of the comfort foods she had enjoyed growing up. As she sat on the sofa attempting to eat, she released a soft sigh of relief and started humming "Amazing Grace." She sang out loud when she got to the line, ". . . and grace will lead me home."

After taking another small bite of her sandwich, Grace noticed the chill in the air was more than she liked, so she got up and walked to the hallway leading to the back of the house. She spotted the thermostat and after she switched the lever to the on position, she heard the humming of the furnace, followed by the smell of warm, musky air coming through the vents.

She was happy that they'd agreed to keep the utilities on at the house. She knew they were holding onto the property for memory's sake despite disagreements about who was most responsible for the bills. She raised a brow as she thought about how her family felt it should be her because of her income. Over the years, that mindset had angered her. But, she let that thought fade away as her reason for being home resurfaced. After the heat was on full blast, she went back to the sofa, looked at the remainder of her food and decided she couldn't eat any more.

She eyed an old photo album sitting on a sagging wooden slat in a bookcase near where her dad's old recliner used to be stationed. The photo album was well preserved given the dampness in the air. After all of her years of returning to the house, she didn't remember the album being there, and it was an album from her early years, no less. She gazed around the room and wondered if she had a ghost or an angel there taunting her. She decided she would ask Hanna if maybe she had placed it there.

She started flipping through the sticky pages as she walked over to the couch and fell back into her cushioned resting place, letting out a deep cough. Her page turning stopped when she saw a picture that she loved. It was their family vacation photo from Biloxi. In the Polaroid, she, Sara, Hanna, and Samuel were all under the age of twelve. Grace's lips and spirit smiled when she saw her pigtails standing out like antlers on the sides of her head. She and her two sisters looked like triplets born years apart, in matching rainbow-colored short sets with identical sandals laced up to their knees. Ten-year-old Samuel stood off to the side in a muscle man pose, wearing a blue tank top, blue-and-white vintage nylon basketball gym shorts, tube socks, and white high-top tennis shoes. *Boy, he was scrawny.* She laughed through a cough and picked up her juice to take a big gulp but spewed some of it onto her lap.

Placing the album on the sofa, she went to the kitchen, wet a paper napkin with cold water, and began wiping the juice off her jeans as she recalled the trip. It was one of their best family vacations. Her dad wanted them to see how white the sandy beaches had fared and how the Gulf Coast had been rebuilt a year after Hurricane Camille devastated the Gulf in 1969. They'd stayed at the Beachcomber Hotel where the smell of boiled shrimp was everywhere and there were seashells for days. Back then, to her, Biloxi was like Shangri-La.

After returning to the sofa, she flipped through a few more pages in the photo album. She turned a page and saw her high school prom picture. Wearing a powder blue floor-length dress, she posed like a debutante next to Sidney Wright, her best male friend in high school. With his hands on her waist and hers on his, they certainly looked awkward enough, she thought. *Lord, why in the world did I think a black girl could pull off a Farrah Fawcett feathered hairdo?* Her smile dropped as she wondered if she would be there for Patrice's prom. She quickly turned the page.

She then saw a photo from her medical school graduation and could almost feel her excitement all over again. *Look at my larger than life four-foot-eleven-inch granny in her oversized blue church hat! She was such a cutie. There's Mama, wearing her Sunday's best and Daddy, standing tall. They were some proud-looking folks. What I wouldn't do to have them here right now.*

She closed the album and tried to conjure up the days of her youth to counterbalance her current burden. She summoned her childhood home to bring some peace of mind. She had witnessed patients during her career who chose to reflect on unmet goals and regrets as they faced potentially life-altering illnesses. She certainly had regrets but didn't want that to be her guide on this trip.

CHAPTER 17

She got up from the couch to toss her bag of remaining food into the garbage bin under the kitchen sink. She sat her juice on the kitchen counter for later. It was time to take a much-needed stroll through the place that had been her refuge for sorting out issues when she was younger. *Could it help me now?*

After Grace closed the cabinet doors under the sink, she walked casually through the family room to the back section of the house and imagined seeing herself running up and down the hallway directing her motorized jeep in and out of rooms. She stopped as she thought of her dad, Pastor Lester Wilson, a king-sized chocolate-brown man whom she believed was her ultimate protector. She could almost see him walking in the direction of her parents' bedroom. In her mental picture, his shoulders were slumped from exhaustion. He was wearing his favorite brown Stetson hat and a gray-and-brown pinstripe suit. She inhaled deeply in hopes of detecting even a slight whiff of his cologne. Following the imagined figure down the hallway as she had done so many times as a child, she could see him lay his hat on the bedside table, hang his jacket in his closet, unlace shoes, and stretch out in a wingback chair in the room as he had done so many times in the past.

His silent shadowy figure felt real in some ways as he wasn't a man of many words in social settings. When he did speak, everyone listened. She recalled having heard adults say that her daddy sure knew how to preach and had a gift straight from God to rightly divide God's Word. Her lips curled as she thought of the 1980s' Wall Street heavyweight E. F. Hutton's commercial. The whole room would become quiet because *when E. F. Hutton talks, people listen.* That's how people responded to her dad. They were always hoping to get a nugget of wisdom from him. She closed her eyes in hopes of making her sense of hearing keener. She imagined she could hear him preaching.

"Church," he would say. "You need to love the skin you're in. That's especially true for you young people. How can you say you love an all-knowing God, a God who made you, and not love yourself? He made you and loves you just as you are. Your skin tone doesn't make you less worthy. God sees the heart of mankind. So, if your heart is sick and is in need of a healing, go to God in prayer. He's the answer. All of our help comes from the Lord!"

Grace particularly remembered one of her favorite sermons, where he preached about "the wheat and the tares," when she was seventeen years old. "Leave Them Alone!" She could hear him saying in his booming voice as he preached about passing judgment on others. He moved on from the tares to the example of the woman who had anointed Jesus's feet. The disciples had been offended because of her sinful lifestyle and because they thought she was wasting expensive perfume by pouring it on Jesus's feet. They didn't see her as being worthy of being in Christ's presence and wanted her tossed out of the house. But Jesus taught them about true worship and servitude through this woman.

She remembered the sermon so vividly because around that time, she had been accused of being judgmental by one of her friends, so she paid close attention.

"As human beings, we spend so much time judging and picking people apart as though we know who is righteous in God's eye," her father had said. "God is the one who will do the separating, not us. Why do you point your finger at a woman on the street who you say has lived a dishonorable lifestyle or that man who can't put the bottle down? Who are you to say how wrong they are? If you had walked the journey they had to walk, you may have made the same or worse choices. Don't judge their responses to their life's pains and struggles. Instead, get on your knees, pray for them, and applaud them. They're still here and didn't choose to take their own lives. No, they have chosen to stay in the race and see it to the end. Get up from where you are and go to your brother or sister and offer them help and hope through Jesus Christ."

Sunday after Sunday, people would come in large numbers to hear what he had to say. Standing in her parents' bedroom, she remembered how she looked to her father with admiration. She needed him so much now. She was always proud of her dad because many African-American men in her local community seemed to struggle with self-esteem. *Yas'sam* and *no'sah* rolled off their tongues with such ease. But that wasn't the case for Pastor Wilson.

He had been educated at Bishop College in Marshall, Texas. Light would sparkle in his eyes as he would tell her, "Bishop was a college founded by the Baptist Home Mission Board as a way to educate us Negro Baptists, beginning in the late 1800s. But, in trying to just get us a little knowledge, we learned the value of family and our heritage. At Bishop, we were allowed to debate the future of the Negro race and were taught to speak out against injustices, whether it was racism or any other social atrocity."

She recalled him preaching with great force from the pulpit time and time again about the importance of education. He taught that the Negro shouldn't depend on a government system to take care of them. He would say that being of strong character would move the Negro race much further than muscle and brawn. He always managed to use the Word of God as his guide as he delivered his social gospel message.

She smiled as she thought about how at home, he always encouraged her to hold her head high. She felt warmth envelop her as she could almost hear him say that they had chosen her name because of their faith in a gracious God who had chosen her for a precious destiny. Being back at her Mississippi home allowed Grace to rehearse events and moments that helped shape her. She had been labeled as a strong woman by her family, friends, and coworkers but now she felt as though her strength was gone. She needed encouragement. She hoped the lessons taught and learned within those walls could come to her rescue now.

CHAPTER 18

Grace glanced around the almost empty room and took a deep breath. She walked across the floor and sat in her mother's white wooden rocking chair. Flakes of paint peeled under the tips of her fingers. As she rocked back and forth, she thought about the phrase *gracious God* and how it meant different things to different people. Her parents were open about God's grace in their lives and often shared their experiences. For her mom, the stories often centered around the events of Grace's birth. *She always called me her miracle baby.*

Two weeks before her due date and during a terrible storm which knocked out the phone line, Grace's mom went into labor while home alone. After she managed to drive herself to the hospital, she was told that the baby was a breech and likely wouldn't survive. Her mom said that's when she called on God and asked Him to give her a much-needed miracle. When Grace was delivered and her mom heard a faint cry, she knew it was God's grace that had kept them both alive. Her parents agreed to name her Grace and to always remind her of the grace that had been shown to them on that day.

Her dad, on the other hand, would say that it was nothing but God's grace and mercy that allowed him and his younger brother to survive a Klan attack when they were children. He would repeat that story many times, often quoting Howard Thurmond, saying, 'Death by violence at the hand of nature may stun the mind and shock the spirit, but death at the hands of another human being makes for panic in the mind and outrages the spirit."

Grace's dad grew up in Raymond, Mississippi, in the 1930s and '40s. It was there that he witnessed his grandfather's lynching in 1941. An angry group of white men stood outside his grandfather's house yelling, "Nigger, get out here!" Her father's face would sadden as he talked about how the men dragged his grandfather out of his own home to kill him.

He and his brother feared they would be killed, too. She remembered her dad saying that Papa Wilson, his grandfather, had been accused of stealing two bales of hay from a white farmer. But according to her dad, the story was the exact opposite. The white farmer had actually stolen from Papa Wilson several times in the past and Papa was fed up about it that day. Papa Wilson told the white farmer he was taking back what belonged to him. Angered by Papa's boldness, the white farmer formed a lynching mob. They murdered him in his own front yard. After they had killed him, the men yelled to her dad and uncle that they were going to be next. Fortunately, before they could come back into the house for them, the sheriff arrived and told the men to move on.

Her dad always angrily noted that no one was arrested for the murder. The sheriff told her dad and his brother to run home and tell their mama to send somebody to take care of Papa's body. He would say over and over that it was a shame before God that nobody was arrested and the law didn't care.

After that event, he began to pray to God for justice for his family. He said he didn't really understand grace then, but he wanted justice to be done and those men to be punished. But, during his time at Bishop College, he was enlightened about God's grace and what unmerited favor really meant. He realized that God cared for all who are called according to His name, no matter who they were, what race they were, or what they had done. His training had taught him that everybody was a sinner and needed God's grace. He began asking God to show his entire family that grace, and he never stopped asking.

Many years later, the white farmer and a few of his Klansmen friends were sent to prison and her dad felt justice had been served. But he also prayed for those men, that God would show them His grace in the end. He would say, "Now, if God granted grace to me, surely I can show grace to somebody else. Oh, bless His name."

Maybe her parents were sending a message. Remembering what she had already come through and what they had experienced, she hoped she was being told that she would make it through her journey with cancer.

CHAPTER 19

G race got up from the chair in her parents' room and walked down the hallway toward the opposite side of the house. She ran her fingers along the outdated velveteen, lavender-and-beige chandelier themed wallpaper that her mom cherished. She feared touching it as a child because *if you dirtied it, you cleaned it*, her mom would demand—and with a toothbrush, no less. But now that same wallpaper with its braille-like quality was a comforting tactile component of her old home.

Grace stopped at her mom's old sewing room, which was once Samuel's bedroom. She envisioned her mom, a medium-framed, somewhat overweight, fair-skinned woman with long wavy hair. Wearing horn-rimmed oval glasses, her mother could often be found sitting at the sewing machine, tailoring a dress from a McCall's pattern. Grace smiled as she touched a button she had accidentally painted into the windowsill many years before. The room had been in desperate need of a fresh coat of paint and Grace had taken it upon herself to surprise her mom by painting it one day. The encased button was the star of that painting escapade. It was left in place to memorialize the button's last day and was a recurring joke in the family.

The warmth reemerged and enveloped her as she thought about how her mom was essentially the "block mom" before the term became a common saying in the Black community. She was always asking the neighborhood children if they had enough to eat and how their schoolwork was coming along. She really lived out the African proverb about village life. For her mom, having bushels of peas or butter beans sent home from a small church as a method of payment for her daddy's revival preaching services meant she had plenty to share with as many as she could. If the Jitney Jungle had a good sale on milk, her mom would buy extra just in case somebody else needed some.

Grace stood at the window and drew a heart in the condensation forming on the pane. She wished she could evoke her mom's words of wisdom but couldn't conjure up a thing. *Somehow, Mom seemed to always know what to tell me about the uncertainties in her life.* She leaned forward, lowering her head onto her crossed hands on the windowsill and took a deep breath. All at once, she began to convulsively cough, cry softly, and rock from side to side.

After a few seconds, she stood up, smeared the drawn heart, dried her hand on her jeans, and wiped away her tears. In some way, maybe she had screwed up by not doing breast self-exams regularly or relying on a mammogram as her safety net. She could almost hear Shelley say how roughly ten to twenty-five percent of lesions are overlooked on mammograms.

I'm a doctor, for Christ's sake, and this happened to me. If only I'd found this out sooner! She looked back at the smeared window through teary eyes before walking out of the room.

Heading for another bedroom off the hallway, she stopped and looked back through the doorway of the family room into the kitchen. She could see a hint of the sloped driveway through the window on the far end of the kitchen. She stopped, because she heard a scratching sound against the window. When she focused, she noticed a fingerlike projection from a branch of a birch tree moving back and forth on the windowpane. As she fixated on the branches, she thought about the nights during the summers when all of the kids on the block would hang out on that slanted slab of concrete.

Back then, her dad had made it clear that the Wilson crew, as he called them, had to be in the house by sundown. She recalled that her mom would give them leeway from time to time when they begged to stay out late with their friends, but only when their dad wasn't home. Her mom's main stipulation was that they had to stay close to the house. On Bible study nights, they pushed the limit when they didn't attend service. She recalled that they usually expected their dad to be late coming home on those nights, so they loitered close to the sloped driveway. They nested near a streetlight right by the house to be sure they had ample time to make a quick break for the door before he pulled up. She smiled through her tears as she thought about the fact that all the kids in the community seemed to have built-in radar for *Pastor's car.*

Grace smiled as she remembered that on one evening, they all missed the signal of the headlights, usually spotted two blocks away. When they saw the headlights dart onto their street, they all scattered like bugs being sprayed with insecticide. A few friends jumped over the fence into the neighbor's yard to hide and a couple more followed them into the house, making their escape through the patio door and scurrying through a side gate before they could be seen. None of them wanted to hear a sermon after getting caught.

Years later, her mom told her that her dad knew what they were up to all along. She once told Grace that he had even laughed when he thought of them scrambling as though they were moving to the orchestral interlude "Flight of the Bumblebee" when they sensed his presence. Her mom let her know that her dad was primarily concerned about his family's safety. He knew that as long as they were close to home, they would be safe.

"Mama, I'm here," Grace said aloud. "I'm as close as I can be to home. Where is my safety?"

CHAPTER 20

Grace resumed her walk down the hallway and entered the room that she had shared with her sister Naomi for years. She looked at a penciled etching on the wall near the closet door, *A+ kid*, a nickname she had been given in junior high school by her classmates. Another fit of dry coughing overtook her as she ran her index finger over the letter. She thought about Patrice's concerns about being placed in the gifted program and how insignificant that all seemed right now. She didn't care if her kids made the best grades or were at the top of their class, she just wanted them to be happy, feel secure, and have their mom around for a while longer.

Grace thought about the fact that she had always been a high achiever but was aware that her mom was a big part of her academic success. She had been the only one of her siblings that her parents felt they could afford to send to a Catholic high school, or at least that was what she was always told. *Grace, you have great potential, and the Catholic school will be good for you,* her mother used to say. But she also recalled her dad shaking his head as he opened his bank statement showing insufficient funds while he was sitting at their round kitchen table with an uneven leg propped up by a couple of wooden shims. She once overheard her dad asking whether it was right for them to continue to put a strain on their finances just to pay for what he felt was overpriced tuition at her school. But then her mother would say, *Lester, don't you know that God will make a way?* But Grace also knew that for her mom, the teacher, good grades and where a child went to school seemed to be what mattered most. *She so desperately wanted me to be competitive at any college that accepted me for admission.* She sighed when she thought about how she complained about not being able to get a car like her other high school friends, whined about the ugly uniforms at her Catholic school, lamented all too often that she had too much school work, and was embarrassed that her friends' parents seemed to have more than her parents did. She could see herself in Patrice. *I was pretty selfish.*

As she eyed a tarnished gold medal attached to a fading first-prize blue ribbon on a shelf in her old closet, she went over and picked it up. She read the engraving and saw that it was a medal from a science fair competition from high school. That ribbon meant so much to her mom, who would often remind her that a Negro child had to always be the best at whatever she did to even be considered at White colleges. Her mom thought that if a Negro girl could make it at a White college, she could write her ticket anywhere she wanted to go in life.

As she squeezed that ribbon in her hand, she thought about how differently she and Stewart had reared their kids. Although she could see the good of her mother's advice in her life, she could also see the instances where it appeared to backfire by impacting her and her siblings' self-esteem from time to time. She sighed when she thought about the relationship between her younger sister, Naomi, and their mom. Naomi thought their mom was especially hard on her because she didn't do as well in school. Naomi preferred singing and she had been praised often at church because she sang like a nightingale.

Grace had once overheard Naomi tell Sara, who was much older than Naomi, that she didn't understand why Mama was so mean to her. Sometimes she thought Mama didn't like her, let alone love her.

Grace recounted how Sara acted like a surrogate mother to Naomi, oftentimes coming to Naomi's rescue. Once, after Naomi received a failing grade on her final book report during her tenth-grade year, Sara told their mom something to the effect that not everybody could be Grace and she needed to stop pitting Grace against Naomi. In essence, lighten up! Her mom's response still rang clear in her head when she said, *Look, if I require the children in my class to do good work, my own kids have to go further and do great work. Do you hear me?* And with those words, the conversation was over.

Now Grace realized that she and her sisters were unfair in their assessment of their mother. After years of being a parent, Grace couldn't help but feel compassion for her mom. Dealing with Patrice's rollercoaster emotions and Chris's possible attention deficit issues was hard for her. She realized that not unlike her mom, she had likely made many mistakes in her children's eyes. She hoped they would someday understand that she was handling matters the best way she knew how. And Grace surmised that when her mom had taken strict disciplinary stances, it was for what she thought was in her children's best interest. Her mom was drawing from her own knowledge of the world and was trying to prevent them from having to go through trials that she had lived through herself. But back then, none of them could see that. They hadn't taken the time to notice how their mom had pushed Naomi more than any of them in vocal, piano, and clarinet lessons. Grace thought about how it seemed that Naomi sang more powerfully after their mother's death. It was almost as though Naomi hoped their mom could hear her songs in heaven and would be pleased.

Grace furrowed her brow and heaved a heavy sigh. How she longed to tell her mom how wonderful and wise she was! When she'd had the opportunity to do it, she had been too young to put those feelings into words. So much for no regrets, she thought. That was surely one.

"Mama, if you can hear me," she said, "know that I love you and I'm sorry that I didn't always appreciate you the way I should have."

Standing in that empty room, her loneliness covered her like a cold blanket. She so missed her mother's touch and caressing words. She surmised that her mom had given her all, not only for them, but for other people, too, without fanfare or recognition. She found comfort in knowing that her mother and father's love for her was genuine and pure in her eyes. Feeling a longing to lay her head on her mom's lap, Grace looked down at the medal again and stuffed it in her back pocket.

CHAPTER 21

G race walked into the last bedroom, the room that Hanna
and Sara shared as children. She immediately thought
about the breakup letter that Sara had helped her write in that
room to her first childhood boyfriend. The boy was named
Tommy, a gangly, big afro wearing, gap-toothed boy, older
than she. His family had just moved into the neighborhood
when they started liking each other. We all thought that boy
was something, she thought. His cool kid label was pinned on
him because he had a brand-new ten-speed bike. Grace
remembered having stretched the truth so that he would like
her. She had told him she was fourteen when she was really
thirteen. He was fourteen going on fifteen, and the age
difference seemed to be a really big deal then. She
remembered her first quick kiss after he walked her home
from a local convenience store—peck, peck. It was
unimpressive, and she had concluded that kissing wasn't all
that people had raved about.

After a couple of months of *dating*, Grace grew bored
with Tommy because all he talked about was comic books,
bicycles, and food. He seemed as deep as a puddle of water.
But the trouble was—how to tell him that they were through?
During her time of deliberation, Grace asked Sara to help her
write a letter to him, her first *Dear John* letter. She laughed

when she thought about how they started the letter: *To Whom It May Concern.* They had both seen letters written like that and thought it sounded neat. Sara was seventeen and a senior in high school then. Having taken a typing class, Sara told Grace that the letter would look more professional if it was typed. Not really knowing what they were doing, they forged ahead with their plan, using their mom's typewriter.

She smiled softly when she thought about how clueless she was about how to actually write the letter and how clueless Tommy had been when reading the letter on the following day after she handed it to him at his house. She could see him wrinkling his nose, focusing quizzically on the letter, and then asking, "Who is to whom it may concern?" She had to explain the letter to him with her own limited knowledge of who *to whom* was and then walk her boyfriend through their breakup process. She thought, Lord, Sara and me with our use of such an impersonal greeting, and poor Tommy lost in the phrase—it was almost too comical for words! When last she heard, Tommy had become a bicycle repairman. She wondered if he was ever destined to leave his teen years.

As she walked back into the family room and stood in front of the fireplace, she thought about entertainment hour at the Wilson house during her childhood. She and her sisters would pretend to be Diana Ross and the Supremes. Hanna, the second oldest, was always Diana because she sang the best until Naomi was born. Plus, Hanna loved wearing makeup, shiny clothes, and high-heeled shoes. As she smiled, Grace felt as though she could actually see herself with Sara doing the backup doo-wop routine. They would sway from side to side as they sang. She felt like it was just yesterday that they were adolescents dressing up in their mom's Sunday clothes and shoes to put on a show to rival *Showtime at the Apollo*. They would laugh and roll around on the floor as they teased each other about their facial expressions while they were singing. She could almost see Samuel teasing Hanna about the way she closed her eyes and poked out her lips while she sang, telling her that she looked like a fish kissing the glass on a tank. Grace smiled and thought about how they would take the show on road around the corner to their cousin Lisa's house when they felt they had a good production to show off. Lisa and her husband always appeared to be amused by their efforts.

Tears welled up in her eyes again. It seemed that out of nowhere, the breast cancer had come rushing back to her like a tsunami of pain. She thought about how and when she would tell this news to the people she loved so much and had shared this house with her most of their lives. She felt the need to keep Hanna from breaking down and Naomi from being too preachy about why Grace should have been in church more regularly. In the midst of the flood of emotions, she could hear Stewart saying, *Stop trying to manage everybody's feelings*. Those few words caused the winds in her heart to blow even harder, creating a vortex that was trying to pull her entire being with it. She did feel the need to control this situation because she didn't want to cause her siblings any pain. But how was she going to do that? How could she stop the spiral?

CHAPTER 22

Grace turned off all of the lights as well as the heater. After locking the door, she left the house, got into her car, and slowly drove around the block to see the house from all angles. She decided to drive around the city for a while before going to Hanna's. They weren't expecting her until two o'clock and looking at the clock on her dashboard, it was about noon which allowed ample time to do more strolling down memory lane. Having not shared her health issues with anyone in her family besides Hanna and feeling uneasy about how the others would handle the news, she was in no hurry to get there.

As Grace drove around without a decided course, she identified familiar cubbyholes and hangouts. She crossed Northside Drive towards Highway 80 and headed towards the Westside of the city where she spotted the old Town and Country Drive-In Theatre. She pulled off to the shoulder of the road and tilted her head slightly to see the remnants of the old oversized outdoor movie screen covered by dense kudzu. It was on that screen she had seen her first outdoor movie, *Planet of the Apes*, starring Charlton Heston. She recalled that was one of the most fun nights she had ever experienced as a child. Hanging the big box speaker on the window for sound seemed so high tech then. The vision of her sisters and her being allowed to buy popcorn at the concession stand popped into her mind. She marveled at the fact that back then children were allowed to leave the car without parental supervision to venture across the large parking lot to seek sweet and salty treats. She almost glowed as she thought about how the fun outing was such a stretch for her dad, who was a serious man and always seemed to be too busy to spend recreational time with anyone. She had always relished getting to spend quality time with her dad whenever she could. That thought caused her to ask herself if she was that different from her father. Alice had become a significant part of their family because her presence made Grace feel she had someone to fill the void while she worked tirelessly. She thought about Patrice's comments that *Mom's always too busy at work*. Had she been taught her workaholic ways from her dad? She wondered.

She placed the gear in drive again and drove a few more miles, passing the old Robinson Road YMCA. She recalled that YMCA stood out in her past because she had taken swimming lessons at the Y three times and had almost drowned three times. She thought about the fact that she never got the hang of swimming but was happy that Patrice and Chris were great swimmers, an accomplishment that she could pat herself on the back for.

As she traveled through other parts of Jackson, she could see the remnants of the McRae's and Woolworth buildings in the old Westland Plaza where she used to shop with her mom when she was a child. She saw what looked like the shell of a building in the spot where her hairdresser's shop used to be. Seeing one dilapidated buildings after another reminded her that as a child she felt those places would be there forever. What she wouldn't do to have those old haunts come to life, wrap her up, and make her feel the kind of happiness she felt back then. But the reality was that they were gone, and like her parents, they weren't coming back.

Grace spotted the Mississippi Farmers Market on High Street as she rolled along. She hadn't realized she had travelled mindlessly past the Jackson Zoo and old Hawkins Field when she pulled into the farmer's market parking lot. I used to love this place as a child, she thought. The sweet juices from the plump peaches running down her arm on the first bite was a delightful memory.

She saw an elderly gentleman standing in front of a booth with signs for pumpkins, sweet potatoes, tomatoes, butter beans, black-eyed peas, and squash. She decided to take a closer look.

"Did you grow all of this yourself?" she asked.

"Yes, ma'am, these'n come from my farm. Me and my son works together," he said.

"I used to come here years ago when I was a child with my family. We would get apples and oranges before Christmas and lots of different kind of nuts, walnuts, and pecans, mostly. My mom would make the best pecan pies. Things don't seem to taste like they used to."

"That's 'cause all the foods is processed now. Jus' a bunch of junk. If'n I don't raise it, I don't eat it. I'm eighty-six years old and been eating the same thangs all my life. I ain't ever ate at no McDonalds. My grandchil'en and great-grans do all the time, though. It's not good fo' em."

"I'll take some squash, tomatoes, and sweet potatoes, please. My sisters will love them."

"Yes, ma'am, I'll get that bagged up for you."

The cordial man's broken grammar reminded her of her of grandparents and she yearned to get him talking more.

"I grew up in Jackson but left here years ago to go to school. I guess I've been gone for almost twenty years now. Like the food, it seems like Jackson has changed so much, as well."

"Yes, ma'am, some fo' the good and some of it ain't so good. But, we's glad you home," said the gentleman.

"Me, too."

"Hits' always a good thang to be able to come home, ain't it?"

"Yes, it is," said Grace as a tear dropped from one eye.

When he saw her tear, he said, "I'm sorry, I hope I ain't said nothin' wrong."

"No, sir, you have not said a thing out of line. It's just me. I'm just happy to be here," she replied.

Grace toted her bags of purchased produce to her car and thought about the effortless and down-home yet profound way in which the man spoke. His plain and folksy style was a part of her Mississippi upbringing that she loved so much. It reminded her of how simple her life seemed as a child. The days of picking juicy, sweet plums from a neighbor's tree in the hot summer after playing a fun game of softball with her friends on a vacant lot in her neighborhood were so special to her.

As she continued to walk, her pace slowed as reality popped up again. Cancer was in her body and was trying to consume her. Feeling that she had too much to live for, an urgent need to make everything right surfaced. Her thoughts quickly pivoted to Patrice. She could hear Alice say, *I think she's just trying to get your attention.* She made a mental note to listen to Patrice more and give her a platform to express herself in a way she obviously longed for. She stopped and looked back at the old man who was watching her walk away.

She lifted her arm holding her produce and nodded. He slowly nodded back.

She picked up her pace and chaffed inwardly as she thought about how she had allowed her work life to drain her even though she didn't have to press herself as hard as she had. And now cancer had the potential to do the same thing. Staying at the hospital late nights, to the point of exhaustion, had become a part of her every day being. Her ambition had pushed her often away from her family. She felt a deep sadness as the weight of Stewart's rants about their family's needs echoed in her head. She realized that more often than she cared to admit, work won in her ranking of priorities. Patrice's declaration about her busyness seemed to float in circles around her head like a Times Square scrolling marquee, and then she saw her dad looking so tired from his constant preaching engagements. She melded into her dad's worn face.

She tried to imagine what being fully present in her family's lives would look like. She recalled having tried yoga once and hearing her teacher talk about mindful breathing and being present in the moment, which she never completely understood. She felt uncomfortable with having to be still and being instructed to do ridiculous stretches, all the while thinking about all the things she could have accomplished during what felt like wasted time. Her teacher would try to help her let go of her hectic life responses and relax through yoga. She decided to look up that yoga teacher again after she got through surgery and chemotherapy to learn how to be settled long enough to listen.

She focused on the fact that she had to be there when Patrice got to go to her first prom. She even pictured Patrice walking down the aisle with Stewart as he gave her away in marriage. *I have to beat this thing.* My God, Chris and I are bound together in ways that Stewart can never understand. What would Chris do without me? Stewart and I have always referred to each other as soul mates. Have I let him down, too?

CHAPTER 23

When she got to her car, she looked back again, and the man was still watching. She waved again and placed the bags of produce on the rear floor mat. She sat quietly for a few minutes looking at all of the farmers' stands. She asked herself when and how ambition had become such a driving force in her life. She thought about what she believed had been her simple life in Mississippi versus her years of exposure to higher education at Vanderbilt University in Nashville. Her college years brought with them thoughts of excitement, information gathering, emotional growth, spiritual awareness, excessive stress, and ambition. She'd felt like a country bumpkin rubbing shoulders with some of the brightest and richest young people in America during those days.

Grace started the engine and placed the gear shift in drive, slowly stepping on the gas to exit the parking lot back onto High Street. As she drove, she quickly flashed back to her freshman year at Vanderbilt. Being one of three African-American women in the entire dormitory, they formed a bond with race as their primary link. Zora Neal Hurston said it best, "All my skinfolk ain't my kinfolk," which couldn't have been truer in their case. Had the environment been different, they probably wouldn't have been friends.

It was there that she began her association with Shelley, as beautiful back then as she is now. Shelley was tall and thin and always seemed to be impeccably dressed no matter what time of day she was seen. Grace pictured the infamous fire drill in their dorm at two o'clock in the morning in late September, soon to become a recurring joke between the two friends. How was it that all of their dorm mates emptied out of the building that night with their hair going in sixty different directions, thick glasses (never usually seen in the light of day), and various bunny-ruffled pajamas, but not Shelley, she thought. She could almost see Shelley exiting the building with her hair combed perfectly, her makeup appearing to be airbrushed onto her face, and a flowing nightgown that could have been copied from a romance novel cover. Only Shelley could make an exit like that, Grace thought and laughed.

Shelley's responses usually had something to do with a man, like, "Yuh never know when a good-looking man gon' be a'roun."

Despite differing personalities, they had remained relatively close. Grace was the intellectual fixer—or maybe control freak—even back then. Shelley has always been the brilliant beauty.

As she continued to drive along, Grace reflected on how she was often intimidated by her classes at Vanderbilt. Although she had a fighter's fire in her belly back then that propelled her to achieve, the first test she bombed in chemistry almost consumed her to her core. Her lifelong need to perform and succeed was short-circuited by Chemistry 101. She thought about how she cried for days about that grade because it had tossed her into a strange territory: failure. She hadn't known how to bounce back from that.

During that time, her supportive, seemingly omniscient mother reminded her that the Grace she reared was the brightest young woman she knew. She used Grace's traumatic birth as an example of how she had survived against the odds. She encouraged Grace to wipe her tears and get back to studying and tackle the next exam head-on. Naomi had been happy about her misfortune though. During one of her phone conversations with her mom, she heard Naomi say, "Good, it's about time. She finally gets to know what the rest of us feel like."

Grace eventually pulled from her grounded energy and conquered chemistry. But had that event become part of her need to always be the best and put too much on her plate as she tried to be and do all things?

CHAPTER 24

Realizing that she had been lost in thought, Grace was surprised when she saw that she was near the old K-Mart her mom liked because *it was always clean*. She was tempted to park and go inside, but the trash littering the parking lot and tall weeds enveloping the landscape was another indicator that times had changed. As she looked at the K-Mart sign and continued to have thoughts about Vanderbilt, she replayed a vivid, unpleasant memory.

During her sophomore year at Vanderbilt, she was financially strapped. Her lack of money was an embarrassment to her. She shook her head as she considered how her priorities fluctuated then. She was well aware that she had made her way to Nashville by that *grace of God* that her dad talked about so much. But she often sulked about what she didn't have compared to her peers. There was no mad money stored away for road trips or dinners with friends or concerts like the other college kids.

Grace remembered wanting to buy a nice baby gift for her first-born niece back then. Having approximately $100 in her checking account for the remainder of the month, she went to a Target near Vanderbilt and purchased an adorable pink and green dress that she thought was perfect. The price tag read $15 with an additional 20% off, which placed it in her price range; so, she put the dress in her shopping cart.

She recalled turning to face one of Vanderbilt's elite couples, the rich cheerleader, Jan, and her hunky intellectual boyfriend, Ross. Jan had been Grace's dorm mate during their freshman year and often either refused to speak to her or looked through her as though she was invisible when they walked past each other. After saying hello and receiving an acknowledgement, they scurried past Grace and looked back with smirks on their faces. She could almost taste the embarrassing sweat that rolled down the sides of her face in that moment. She felt like a bag lady stuffing tin cans and bargain basement clothing from Target in her basket.

As Grace continued to drive, she realized she was facing what seemed to be a recurring theme that haunted her while she was at Vanderbilt and beyond. She didn't feel she was good enough, even though her parents tried to instill the value of self-worth in her throughout her life. Her family wasn't rich enough and didn't have enough.

She'd first met Jan at her dorm retreat freshman year. Jan was quick to share that her family owned high-rise hotels in New York, Boston, San Francisco, Dallas, and Chicago. She loved to flaunt her wealth. Grace knew enough about Jan's father from the media and was fascinated by his rags to riches story. But her enthrallment soon dissipated when Grace realized Jan chose not to engage in conversation with her as though she wasn't worthy.

Grace sobered as she remembered going home for Christmas that year and sharing the Target event with her mom. Recalling the glum look on her mother's face, Grace remembered feeling worse than she did at that Target. She had wounded her mom. And from her mom's expression,

Grace believed that her mother's eyes said that in spite of all that they had done for her, it wasn't enough. She never talked about the subject again with her mom and never had the guts to rehash the perceived pain. The fact that she had allowed Jan and Ross to make her feel inferior based on their own silly standards stayed with her for some time.

When she discussed it with her dad a few months later, she recalled him reminding her that wealth is a very subjective thing. He said, *In the ghetto, the family with hot meals on the table, a late model vehicle, and kids with clothes from a local department store are often considered rich by those who have less than that. But that very same family would be considered poor in the eyes of the family whose income is in the six-figure category. And that six-figure family would be considered as marginally making it to the wealthiest 2% of America. Remember, your value can't be measured by someone else. God has placed unique abilities in you. Focus on that and not on what other people have.*

The Vanderbilt crowd had a way of putting class and wealth in her face. Realizing that she had not taken all of her dad's wisdom to heart, she thought about her ongoing ambition and drive to succeed. What did it all matter now? As her cancer diagnosis drifted back across her mind, all of those college frivolities seemed so ridiculous. Her health challenge caused her to focus on the fact that sickness equalizes us all. Cancer is no respecter of persons; it has always been an equal opportunity offender.

As she slowly rolled up to a stop sign, she pushed her foot on the brake and focused on the song on the radio. Stevie Wonder was crooning, *Mary wants to be a superwoman / But is that really in her head.* She quickly thought about the exchange between Stewart and her in Mr. Marshall's classroom. Superwoman, yeah right.

CHAPTER 25

Grace turned off of Highway 49 onto Alderman Drive and drove towards Second Baptist Church, her spiritual safe house, where her dad had pastored for thirty-five years. The church never seemed to change. The beautiful deep purples, reds, and blues in the stained glass windows depicted scenes from the ascension and pearly white doves flying heavenward, glimmering and inviting parishioners to come on in.

Her grandmother would say that Second Baptist was a pretty church, but it wasn't her church home. She wanted everyone she talked to at Second Baptist to know that her church home was Bethel Holiness Church in Raymond, Mississippi. Grace remembered how she and Samuel used to laugh as children about that recurring statement. Samuel once asked their mom if their grandma thought that maybe Saint Peter would scratch her name off the roll in heaven because she was cheating on the holiness church by praying with the Baptists. Grace smiled as she thought that unlike her grandma, she felt that her heart belonged to Second Baptist.

While in the parking lot, she saw ladies getting out of their cars with what looked like covered dish items. One of the church ministries must be having a pot luck brunch, Grace thought. She closed her eyes and thought about her days as a regular church member there with choir rehearsals, usher board meetings, and girl scouting events, all taking up what seemed like an inordinate amount of time. Her mama felt like they could never get too much church, although she and her siblings didn't agree.

She opened her eyes as she recalled that each time she returned home from college, her dad always made a big fuss over her at the church. He would say, *Grace, stand up so that everybody can see you. As you all know, my Grace is a pre-med student going to Vanderbilt. How about that?*

He would tell her that all of his children were his treasures, so he took pride in showing them off. Her dad seemed proudest when she was accepted to medical school and made an even bigger fuss over her then, much to her embarrassment.

That memory quickly faded into her father's funeral services at the church which brought back the pain of that loss. Her larger than life hero, her seemingly immortal dad, had succumbed to death and the grave. Although as a physician she had witnessed death in many forms, she wasn't ready when her dad's final breath was taken. She could almost see his casket being rolled out of the church. It was then that her faith or lack thereof felt exposed and bare. As a child, she'd had a solid faith, and this pleased her parents. But somewhere along the way, she had drifted from her need for and her connection to God. Sitting in the parking lot of the church where her religious foundation was laid, she asked herself some questions. The what ifs plagued her, and she couldn't believe how she felt so defeated after all she had accomplished in her life.

What if something goes wrong in the operating room, and I end up with permanent damage so that I can't work?

What if Stewart decides caring for me and the kids is just too much, and he decides to leave? What if I become a burden on my family? What if I die? Her state of uncertainty began to consume her.

Suddenly, Grace heard a knock on her window. It was Mother Jenkins, who had been her Sunday school teacher years before. She had to be at least seventy-five years old now. Mother Jenkins was a beautiful woman whose eyes looked like glossy black marbles perfectly fitted in a worn but velvety soft, well-aged face. Grace quickly opened the car door and jumped out to embrace Mother Jenkins with an all-encompassing hug.

Mother Jenkins said in her sweet southern vernacular, "I thought'ed that was you in that car. You looked like you was in a deep trance or somethin'. I didn't want to bother you, but I said to myself, that chil' looks like she could use one of Mother's hugs. Based on how you squeezed me, I was right." She smiled. "Grace, why don't you come inside with me?"

"I shouldn't because I'm supposed to be at my sister's house and don't want to be late," Grace responded.

But after persistent encouragement, she decided she would to go inside for a moment. Following Mother Jenkins, she stepped into the church gymnasium. Grace waved to a number of women, some of whom she recognized and others she had never seen before. As they entered, Mother Jenkins waved to a few ladies near the serving table and another group of ladies sitting at a circular table in the middle of the room to come over.

"Can y'all come over here, please? Look who I saw out in the parking lot!" shouted Mother Jenkins. "I don't know if all of you remember Grace Wilson? It's sho' good to see her.

Her daddy used to be our pastor for about thirty-somethin' years before he passed on to be with the Lord. I want y'all to say hey to her."

As people moved from various corners of the room to the entrance, Mother Jenkins started telling stories about how Grace and her daddy were inseparable when Grace was a toddler. Grace smiled and began exchanging hugs and hellos with the women.

"Lord, her daddy would have this here chil' with him everywhere, when she was a baby. Sometimes, he even had to hold her while he was in pulpit waiting to preach caus' she was crying so for her daddy," chuckled Mother Jenkins.

"I was a daddy's girl for a while, I guess," said Grace.

Grace recognized Jill Sanders who had been a member of the church since they were children. Jill waved, ran over, and hugged Grace.

"How have you been, Grace? Girl, I haven't seen you in what, three years? You look great. You've lost some weight, haven't you?" asked Jill.

"A little, but I don't want to talk about me. If I'm not mistaken, I believe Hanna told me that you are now the Girl Scouts' troop coordinator at the church?"

"Yeah, can you believe that?"

"You know, when Hanna told me that you were a troop leader, all I could conjure up was how we would stay up all night when we went to camp because we were both so afraid of bugs."

"So, I'm still afraid of bugs, but I make sure my troop gets the indoor rooms at the campsite," giggled Jill.

They laughed and reminisced for a short period and began to wind down their conversation as they heard Mother Jenkins's voice echo across the gym.

"Yeah, I spotted her out in the parking lot. Now Grace's mama, Sista' Wilson, made for sho' her chil'ren was at the church for everything that happened here. Now see, that's what is missing with these young gurls these days," said Mother Jenkins.

Grace crossed back over to where Mother Jenkins was sitting as she waved goodbye to Jill. She asked Mother Jenkins, "Do you mind if I take a walk around the church?"

Mother Jenkins patted her on the back.

"This church will always be yo' church. Anyway, you don't have to ask nobody fo' permission to walk around yo' own house, chil'."

After leaving the gymnasium, Grace walked down a long corridor that led to the sanctuary. She walked up and down a few aisles of colonial styled solid oak pews and then she went to the altar, kneeled, and prayed.

"Dear God, I don't even know where to start. I'm desperate right now. I know I might appear to be a hypocrite because I'm only here because I'm in trouble. You know, I guess I thought I had this life game together. I've depended on my intellect for such a long time. Well, shame on me because science failed me, and I failed myself. Lord, I really hope you're hearing me right now. I just need help and again, I'm sorry. Amen." She made the sign of the cross out of habit as she had done so often during mass at her Catholic high school and then stood up.

Wiping her tears, Grace walked out of the sanctuary and headed down another hallway toward the pastor's study. She approached a wall of portraits of previous pastors of the church, dating back to 1920. Her sadness began to lift as she approached her father's picture. She stopped and stared. Grace saw her dad full of life in his favorite deep purple liturgical robe with three black bars encased in gold piping on the sleeves. As she focused on his deep set, dark eyes, she felt as though he was penetrating her façade.

She began to cry again. "I wish you were here right now, Daddy. I'm just scared." She shook her head at the flurry of emotions.

Just as Grace felt as though she was about to shatter, Mother Jenkins turned the corner. Grace patted her eyes quickly.

Mother Jenkins touched Grace on her back. "We still miss him, too. Yo' daddy was a good man. We lov'ded our pastor."

Grace realized she needed to leave before she broke. Grace told Mother Jenkins that she had to go and pushed past her, running through the set of heavy, metal double doors that were closest to her. She needed air.

CHAPTER 26

Grace ran to her car and started the engine. The radio hummed in the background. She started frantically pressing the arrows on her steering wheel to change the station. She stopped on a country western station when she heard the radio announcer say, *Thank you for listening to Jackson's favorite country station, WJXI. Next up, Tim McGraw and "Live Like You Were Dying."*

More tears began to flow. She listened to the words of the song and realized she was hearing her pain crooned on the airways.

She shifted the gear to drive and rolled away. With her vision obscured by her thick tears, she pulled into the parking lot of a dentist office, only a couple of blocks away from the church. As she listened further, she belted out the chorus in convulsive gasps.

Grace suddenly remembered a patient she had cared for at Emory Hospital in Atlanta, during her first year of residency training. Sue Lim was a twenty-six-year-old Korean woman who was a first-year graduate student at Georgia State University. Grace remembered finding Sue to be soft-spoken, bashful, and friendly. Sue's gums had been bleeding on a regular basis along with the presence of easy bruising. Sue had shared with Grace back then that she had gone to a family practice doctor to have some tests done given the bleeding and because she had felt run down. After that doctor's visit, Sue was contacted by an unknown clerk from her doctor's office letting her know that she needed to go to Emory Hospital Emergency Room immediately, because of some abnormal lab tests.

Why am I thinking of Sue right now? She and Sue were close in age at the time, making her pause even back then. Grace remembered how discussing Sue's medical history with her attending physician frightened her because she had never seen cancer up close in someone around her age. Although so many years had passed, she relived the emptiness in the pit of her gut that she felt as she solemnly stared at Sue and told her that she had acute myelogenous leukemia (AML). Grace had known that AML was a cancer of the bone marrow and that it originated in the white blood cell system and was usually aggressive. She remembered how her heart broke as she read about the terrible prognosis associated with Sue's AML diagnosis, along with all the side effects of the nasty chemotherapy drugs that would be administered.

Grace replayed one of the conversations she and Sue had during her oncology rotation. During her daily patient rounds back then, she often spent more time with Sue than some of her other patients. She had begun to look forward to listening to Sue share her dreams as if she had a whole lifetime to achieve them all. Grace thought about how she never let on to Sue that her life expectancy, according to the textbooks, would be greatly shortened.

Squinting and staring aimlessly at a parked truck in the dental office parking lot, she thought of how Sue loved talking about her culture and how life and death was viewed in her homeland. Sue didn't understand the Americans' fear of dying. Sue told her that death was not a forbidden thing that could be avoided. Sue had been taught as a child that she should do her best in life to achieve all that she could and leave whatever was beyond her control to fate. She had been taught that death was simply a part of life. Sue had told Grace that in her culture, they celebrated a life well lived and a death well died.

Grace recalled how badly she felt when she almost didn't recognize Sue during the time of her next oncology rotation as a second-year resident. At that time, she witnessed a battered woman who had lost her smile and determination after a year of chemotherapy for an unrelenting and relapsing disease. Grace thought about how Sue's hope appeared to have dissipated. Sue told her that she knew she was going to die and she wasn't afraid of death. Sue's unfulfilled wishes echoed in Grace's mind. She had hoped she would be married and have a family someday. And, although her boyfriend hadn't stuck it out with her through her whole illness, she was happy to have known the intimacy of love. Sue had asked the medical team at Emory if she could go home to be with her family in Korea to die. She had given up on western medicine. The oncologists felt her request wasn't realistic based on how sick she was. Sue died during that hospital admission with a couple of her family members at her bedside.

Maybe Sue had visited her memory to remind her that she wasn't alone. She had family and friends that would assist her through this part of her life's journey. She also thought that Sue had come to her as a teacher, reminding her that she should do her level best to live well and leave the death and dying part to God. But she still had an uneasiness about her own personal situation that even Sue's memory couldn't completely abate.

CHAPTER 27

After her long day, Grace finally arrived at Hanna's house around 3:00 p.m. As she pulled into the driveway, willowy smoke rose from the chimney. *Hanna likes her cozy surroundings.* Not long after putting the car in park, Hanna and Sara barreled out the front door and Naomi and Samuel exited the house from the door just inside the garage that led to the kitchen. They each took turns hugging Grace.

"Okay, Ms. Thing, where have you been? We have been trying to call and text you!" snapped Hanna as she released Grace from her hug and scanned her like a skeptical TSA agent.

Naomi exclaimed, "You had better be glad I love you. I was about to leave."

"No, you weren't," Samuel countered. "You practically bit your lip off because you were so worried that something had happened to her."

"Whatever," spouted Naomi.

Looking down at her phone and covering her mouth with her hand, Grace apologized. "I'm so sorry, but I stopped by Dad and Mom's place to check on some things, stopped at the farmers market, and even stopped by the church. I forgot that I'd put my cell on vibrate when I was at the church. I see now that I missed a few calls. Please forgive me."

"I'll consider it," said Naomi, smiling.

"Why were you over by the farmers market? That's out of the way, isn't it?" asked Sara.

"I know. I just did a 'good ole days' kind of thing. I guess I drove around for a few hours. To tell you the truth, I lost track of time. It was quite sentimental," responded Grace.

"Why are we standing outside when there is a perfectly good house waiting for us and with good food, too?" asked Samuel. He grabbed Grace's bag out of the trunk. Grace asked him to also grab the produce from the back seat.

Samuel walked with Grace ahead of Hanna and Naomi and whispered, "You look tired, baby girl. Go inside and take a load off." Then changing his tone abruptly, he humorously asked, "Is Stewart feeding you enough? I don't need to call social services, do I? You look like you're wasting away."

"I do not, Samuel. Stop with the jokes."

"You do look like you have lost a few pounds. Have you been dieting?" asked Sara.

"No, I've had a lot of things going on lately and haven't been eating properly."

"Really, folks, I think we need to let Grace get settled in before she is placed on the witness stand for questioning by the inquisition squad. And, anyway, I was just trying to keep it light, and y'all had to go get all serious on me," said Samuel.

The sisters all laughed, but Naomi rolled her eyes saying, "Enough of your lame stand-up comedy, Sam."

"You have to admit, he does have some good one-liners, every now and then," said Sara.

Grace followed Samuel like a newly arriving hotel guest being escorted by a well-trained bellman. She waited as he stopped briefly at the kitchen and laid the produce on the center island. Then, after passing the family room and a hallway bathroom, they arrived at her assigned guest room, with its sage green walls and French country design that offered cozier surroundings. Samuel placed her duffel bag at the foot of the bed. Hanna followed them to the room and scurried Samuel out.

Grace turned to her. "Thanks for listening to me yesterday. I was a wreck."

"No, you were just fine," Hanna replied. "I'm experiencing a bit of disbelief myself. I can only imagine all of the things going on in your head."

"Yeah, it's kind of like a terrible dream that you can't shake." Grace coughed and took a deep breath.

"Did you try to do too much today, Grace? Do you need to lie down? Do you need some water?" asked Hanna worriedly.

"I'm tired, but I don't want to give anyone a reason to ask questions. You know me, the energizer bunny. Isn't that what you guys have always called me? So, I'll keep going. I'll get something to drink a little later."

Grace and Hanna went back to the kitchen to join the others. Grace sat on one of the high-backed black leather barstools beside the kitchen island. She looked over at the massive spread consisting of grilled pork chops, turnip greens, cornbread, and bubbling macaroni and cheese sitting on the stove across from her. Potato salad, iced tea, and caramel cake were also laid out on the kitchen table in the breakfast nook.

Grace didn't have the heart to tell them she didn't think she could eat much. Instead she said, "Hey, Hanna, can you fix my plate? But make all of the portions small, if you don't mind."

"You are dieting! The Grace I know would have loaded up on everything on this stove. Hanna and I made all of your favorites," said Sara.

"No, no, I promise. I'm not on a diet. I'm sorry, but I ate earlier and I'm still a little full. I didn't expect you guys to go all out for me," Grace responded.

Hanna placed small portions of all of the dishes on a paper plate and placed it in front of her.

"What's your preference for your drink?" she asked.

"Iced tea is fine, if you have some," responded Grace.

"I made the iced tea, so I know it's good," said Naomi.

"Thank God she only made tea," said Samuel and they all laughed.

Hanna sat next to Grace, preparing to eat, when her husband, Glen, and Sara's husband, Alan, entered the house from the garage. Hanna pushed her plate aside and walked up to her husband. "Grace is here."

"Hey, sister-in-law, you look good. How's my friend Stewart doing?" Glen bellowed while hugging Grace.

"He's great, just working too much, not unlike me." Grace then turned to Alan and said hello as they hugged. She looked around the room quizzically. "Hey, Sam, what time do your kids get out of school? Shouldn't you be picking them up about now?"

"School lets out at 3:15pm, but they're spending the rest of the day with my fiancée."

"Your what?" asked Sara.

"Donna and I've been talking about marriage for a little while and I popped the question about a week ago. She said yes."

"Congratulations! You deserve happiness and Donna seems to bring you joy," said Grace.

As everyone joined in congratulating Samuel, Grace thought about how she and her siblings supported him through his nasty divorce and custody battle.

"Do you remember how you vowed to never marry again?" asked Grace. "Look at you now. Boy, you are grinning from ear to ear."

As the conversation swirled around Samuel and his marriage plans, Grace thought about his first wife, Sheila, who had been having affairs off and on right under Sam's nose for the better part of their ten-year marriage. Samuel had been told by friends and co-workers that Sheila had been seen with a man coming out of restaurants and even hotels. He didn't want to face the reality. After their father's death, Samuel began working nonstop, twelve and fourteen-hour days, to get through his pain. After their mom got sick, he sank even further into a workaholic swamp. She shook her head as her own issues of workaholism resurfaced.

Grace remembered an argument she'd had with Sheila three years before about the rumors of her affairs. Sheila said she was bored with her life as a wife to Samuel and hated being a stay-at-home mom. She felt Samuel was never available for fun. Grace told her in no uncertain terms that if she'd gotten off her lazy behind and worked, maybe she wouldn't be so bored.

But Samuel and Sheila's problems went deep. Samuel's workaholic nature, which likely sprouted from his desire to earn his dad's approval, seemed to hinder him from being fully present in his family's lives. *That "fully present" issue keeps showing up.* As hard as her mom appeared to be on Naomi, her dad was even more demanding of Samuel. He ingrained in Samuel the idea that a man had to work and work hard to gain respect in this world. Her brother took that lesson to heart.

"Man, Donna is a good woman and not hard on the eyes, either. That Sheila was a piece of work, though," said Glen, laughing.

Hanna punched Glen in his arm. "In all seriousness, Sam, Glen and I are happy for you and not just because Donna is a pretty girl. I pray this marriage is forever."

Everyone nodded quietly.

"Who are you telling? Donna wants to have the ceremony in January or February. I know it's short notice, but we're not young kids. It'll be simple," said Samuel.

Grace smiled but considered that she might not get to be at the wedding depending on how things went with her treatment.

"Hey, get back to your food, guys. I don't want anyone blaming me for cold chow," said Samuel. He encouraged Grace to taste the greens. "You know Sara used my secret recipe. So don't let her try to trick you into thinking that this is all her handiwork."

"Thanks, guys, I'll eat a little now. But I suspect I'll get the late-night munchies and will fix another plate then," Grace said.

"Okay," said Samuel.

After everyone had finished eating, Hanna, Grace, and Sara began cleaning the kitchen. Hanna encouraged Grace to rest, but Grace insisted she wanted to help. Once the kitchen was cleaned, the ladies joined everyone else in the family room where the men were drinking decaffeinated coffee.

Hanna got everyone's attention, "Guys, Grace wants us all to meet at the old house in the morning to share some news."

"What news?" asked Samuel, turning to face Grace.

"It's just something that I'd feel more comfortable talking about at Dad and Mom's old place."

"What time tomorrow? I like to sleep in on Saturdays," said Naomi, smiling.

"Maybe around eight or nine. Is that okay with everyone?" asked Grace.

"Oh, Lord, she must be getting ready to run something. I'll be there, of course," said Naomi.

Grace smiled and looked past Naomi as she tried to keep her composure.

"Okay. It could be fun for all us to be over there, tomorrow. So, let's nail down a time," said Sara.

"Eight o'clock," said Grace.

"That should be fine," said Sara. "But, since we're all here now, you can't tell us?"

Grace fidgeted in her chair and was about to speak, when Hanna interrupted in an attempt to sway the conversation.

"I know we just cleaned the kitchen, but would anyone like dessert? We have pound cake and a chocolate cake."

"I'll have a slice of chocolate and pound cake," said Naomi, laughing.

They all headed back to the kitchen and ate varying sizes of cake slices on paper plates.

Samuel ate his cake hurriedly.

"I'll be there in the morning," he said. "I need to head home and make sure the kids are settled. I don't want them running Donna off just yet," he went on to say, laughing.

The sisters said their goodbyes to Samuel before going on to reminisce and swap stories late into the night.

CHAPTER 28

After everyone left Hanna's place, Grace and Hanna sat at the kitchen table and Grace replayed what she had experienced prior to the diagnosis.

"Grace, how are you holding up? Aren't you afraid?"

"I'm terrified."

Grace went on to tell her about how she prayed at the altar and later fell apart when she saw their dad's portrait in the church hallway.

"I've just been so panic-stricken lately," she admitted. "You know me, I prefer being the fixer. It's usually me bringing clarity to people's health concerns. But ever since I fell down those stupid steps at work and found out about the cancer, everything has been spinning out of control. My emotions have been all out in the open which is very discomforting.

"Being at the church was weird in a way, too. I don't know how long it's been since I kneeled at an altar. Not that I'm anti-church, but I haven't been at church regularly since before Daddy died. Stewart has tried to hold down the spiritual front at our house for years with the kids, but I just haven't been interested in going. I know I'm rambling. But, I guess what I'm getting at is that it felt surprisingly good to pray that way."

"Well, I'm glad you prayed at Second Baptist today," Hanna said. "Over the years, I'd like to believe that I've developed a closer connection to God, so I pray a lot. Grace, you're a smart woman who's achieved a lot in your lifetime, but I believe we all need God. I mean, you can't reason away everything. Sometimes you have to seek a higher power for direction. That being said, I'm happy you were led to stop by the church. But we've done enough talking for tonight. You look tired. Why don't you go to bed?"

"I will. But do you think anyone has a problem with going to Dad and Mom's place tomorrow?"

"Not at all. I think they're curious about why you wanted to talk there rather than here, but Naomi thinks you're going to tell us that you've been chosen to become president of the medical school or something like that," said Hanna, laughing. "I haven't said anything to them."

"Okay, I appreciate that."

"How do you plan to broach the subject?" asked Hanna.

"I guess I'll just go with the flow, but I don't really know. I won't expect us to be there too long before I say something. I hope."

"Okay, but get some rest. We have to get an early start in the morning. Plus, I don't know about you but I need my beauty rest."

"Please, you know that's not true. You've always been beautiful."

They hugged one another and said goodnight. After Grace reached the guest bedroom, she began unpacking her bag. She placed an organic cotton, black, knee-length jacket, a white short-sleeved tank, and black jeans on the back of an oversized chair across from the bed. Running her hand over the clothes, she attempted to smooth out any wrinkles to avoid having to iron in the morning.

Grace then sauntered back across the room to continue unpacking. She removed a baby blue cotton flannel nightgown with an open neckline. Grabbing the nightgown by the sleeves, she shook it out with a quick snap and accidentally dropped it to the floor near the side of the bed. As she bent over to pick it up, she gasped and felt lightheaded. She sat on the foot of the bed to steady herself. After a couple of minutes, she proceeded to remove her clothes from a seated position and then walked to the en suite bathroom to take a quick shower.

Wrapped in a large bath towel, she looked down at her nightgown across the room, still lying on the floor. Rather than risking feeling lightheaded again, she sat on the bed and used her toes to retrieve her gown from its place of repose. Once she secured it, she pulled the gown over her head.

Grace crawled from the foot of the bed towards the headboard and pulled back the neatly tucked down comforter and white Egyptian cotton sheets. Anticipating its softness, she planted herself in the center of the bed and stretched out for her purse resting on the bedside table. She sat back up and searched through the abyss of her purse and found her comb. Using the comb to detangle her hair, she parted her hair down the center from front to back. She plaited her hair into two thick braids and then laid back on the bed again after turning off the lamp on the neighboring nightstand.

Although she was drained, her eyes remained open as she looked into the darkness, her past memories illuminating the room like flashes of light. In that light, she could almost feel the warmth and see the rays of the sun, as she harkened back to that summer of 1989. It was in that year she emigrated from Jackson, Mississippi, with all of its genteel southern ways and false delicacies to Atlanta, Georgia, and its high-rise buildings, haze, and traffic. She remembered that the air was so hot and muggy in Atlanta that year that it seemed impossible to find breathing space. But the climate's sticky unpleasantness was blown away by her cool yet leery confidence at the start of her internship at Emory University.

Apprehension about her health invoked a familiar fainthearted and insecure feeling not unlike what she felt as a 'newly crowned' doctor thrown into the *bowels* of Grady Hospital, Emory's affiliated hospital. The unpredictability of life in those uncertain times bore similarity to how she now felt. She had a lot of "what if" questions back then about whether she had what it took to make it through the rigorous hours of training and patient care. But now her what ifs were about the rigors of chemotherapy. Could she bear it? She'd taken care of many cancer patients, including her parents, but what would it be like for her to be in a hospital bed?

Grace had hoped she would beat the cancer odds. After all, she had studied cancer genes and carcinogens during her career. She had read about anticancer diets and had made lifestyle modifications accordingly. She felt she had learned what it would take to not develop cancer or even reverse her chances of getting it, even if she did have some genetic predisposition. But all of her efforts hadn't been enough. Breast cancer had entered her life, exposing her deficiencies, just as Grady Hospital had done so many years before.

CHAPTER 29

As she continued to stare into darkness, Grace thought about how she had stood against adversity many times in her life. She had been up for the challenge, every time. But for whatever reason she felt so defeated now. She thought of her challenges growing up in Mississippi in the nineteen sixties and seventies, on the edge of the Civil Rights Movement. She had understood racism to a certain degree, but that racial disparity many times caused her to question her belief in her own abilities. She remembered that her parents often impressed upon her what the racial climate in Mississippi meant for a young black girl, which was why they had encouraged her to go as far as she could academically.

She started softly humming Nina Simone's "To Be Young, Gifted and Black." That song had become her mantra when she was twelve years old at Clements Junior High located in Clinton, Mississippi, on the outskirts of Jackson. It was there that she was one of a handful of black children in her daily class rotation block. Though she lived in an all-black neighborhood, she attended the predominantly white county school for her elementary learning and later a predominantly white Catholic high school. In spite of making all A's during her first year at Clements Jr. High School, her teachers, who were all white except for her physical education teacher who was African-American, didn't trust her work. To her, it always seemed to be a game of cat and mouse with her teachers trying to trip her up.

Many years ago, Grace was inducted into the Junior National Honor Society. It was significant because she had achieved a major accomplishment by making all A's, which no one else had done that year. She remembered sitting in the school auditorium, hardly able to contain herself. She proudly waited, in her newly purchased, pink, double-knit, knee-length dress with baby blue piping around the collar and pockets, for her name to be called. Her mom was in the audience, ready to root her on.

But Grace cringed when she recalled her principal, who appeared to make a big deal out of the fact that only one student had a grade point average of 98% and had all A's that year. Then she could almost distinctly hear him say, *Come on up, Grace Johnson.* Grace Johnson was the school's head cheerleader who had never made grades good enough to be considered for the honor society, and she was white. Grace recalled feeling hurt but determined. She remembered quickly standing up and accepting her award because *she knew who she was and what she had earned.* Several of the teachers commented to her during the following week that they thought it was kind of funny that she stood up even though her name wasn't actually called. One teacher asked her what she would have done if it really was Grace Johnson he was calling to come up on stage and not her.

"Grace, it would have been so embarrassing," the teacher had said.

Grace had respectfully said that she knew it was supposed to be her because she knew that she was the only one who had made that accomplishment.

Then, Grace thought about Mrs. Galley, a history teacher, who would say *niggras* when they were studying the era of slavery. Whenever Mrs. Galley saw the word *negroes*, she would say that it is to be pronounced *niggras* and insisted that was the way Grace was supposed to say it as well. At the time, Grace shared her frustration with her dad, telling him that Mrs. Galley was wrong to pronounce negro like that and she was wrong for trying to make her feel like she was dumb for pronouncing it correctly.

"Grace, baby, you can't change the way anyone thinks. What I want you to do is overlook prejudice and prove people wrong. Strive to be the best and the brightest. You know that you're not a nigger. Remember, you are young, gifted, and black."

He would have her repeat that phrase over and over. Not long after her conversation with her dad, she heard the Nina Simone song which stuck with her. She smiled as she remembered graduating from junior high school with honors in a mostly segregated, but forcibly integrated, South.

She'd made a promise to herself after her high school graduation that she would never go back to Mississippi to live unless she could truly bring about some level of change there. But as fate would have it, she had come back for short extended periods of time to help care for her parents during their illnesses. Now here she was again. The place that she so wanted to get away from all those years before was where she escaped to for comfort. Facing the memories of her past made her appreciate the life she had built with her husband and children in Knoxville.

CHAPTER 30

Although she was exhausted, sleep didn't appear to be a part of the night's agenda. She couldn't believe how her thoughts gushed in waves and appeared to overflow onto her cotton pillowcase. She'd paid so little attention to being alive before cancer's threat of death. It's easy to take for granted being able to get up every day and live a relatively healthy life. The threat of death seemed to have given her the code to open a vault for entry into her past.

She thought again about her former patient, Sue Lim, and Sue's beliefs about life and death. *Sue was one of my teachers.*

Hoping to catch some sleep, Grace tried to change her focus and turn her thoughts to God and the messages He wanted her to receive. Was He testing her faith? Was He saying, *Open your eyes, you poor, lost soul?* Or was He jumping up and down, yelling, *I've been sending you warning signs all along, but I had to put up a roadblock to finally get your attention?*

For so many years, she'd fixated on what appeared to be important, like climbing the career ladder, but it was all so insignificant now. The fact that she was always looking for one more thing to do, whether it be another hospital committee, volunteering at the kid's school in a narrow space of time carved out a jam-packed day, the never-ending hospital charting and rounding, or doing household chores.

Even though she paid someone else to do them, she did them herself because she didn't want Alice to think she was lazy. When did she become such a robot? Had she been focused on gaining another title and fixing everybody else's problems that she overlooked her own brokenness?

She was competing with non-competitors to be declared the greatest wife, mom, sister, friend, and doctor, all while scrambling on a hamster wheel of approval that went nowhere. *Was that my baggage from Mama and Daddy? They meant well by trying hard to push me to be the best so that I would be deemed worthy by White America.* Their push, that drive, had become a barrier for Samuel, too. His workaholic issues had already caused problems in his marriage.

She shook her head as she soberly thought about how this affliction, cancer, had entered her life and become an unwanted teacher. What would be the lesson plan? Would the curriculum include subjects like the importance of rest or discerning what matters most in life or unlocking the secret to having meaningful quality time? She hadn't signed up for the classes but was being forced to take the test.

As she sat up in bed, pulled the covers around her neck, and stared into the blurry darkness, she tried to focus on what looked like the frame of a wall hanging in her room. Suddenly, a young man named Chester, a patient that she cared for during her residency training at Grady Hospital, popped into her mind. He hadn't crossed her mind in years.

Chester had been diabetic since childhood and was insufferably noncompliant with medical therapy. He had never taken his insulin properly. He had eaten candy like it was his medication and frequently missed his dialysis appointments. Grace remembered that she thought he had a death wish because of the way he chose to live. Chester had already had one leg amputated above the knee, was on hemodialysis, and was legally blind at the age of thirty-four.

Her eyebrows raised as she recalled how close she'd gotten to loathing Chester. To her, he was a depressive, under-educated black man who appeared to be mad at the world. She lay back on the pillow and looked up at the ceiling. She began to shake as she coughed and felt her smothering sorrow build up again as she remembered her worst encounter with Chester during her last year of residency.

On an evening when Chester was determined to leave the medical unit against medical advice, she had been called by a nurse to inform her that Chester was trying to *escape*. She had walked onto the unit expecting to confront the usually belligerent man for whom she had so much disdain, but that day he appeared to be a stoic, apathetic individual, sitting on the floor having fallen from his bed without his prosthesis. He seemed unfazed by his bruises and scraped elbow. His gown was no longer covering his naked body. She remembered a man who chose to risk his life, despite knowing he was suffering from diabetic ketoacidosis, congestive heart failure, and was in need of further hemodialysis. Chester was determined to get out of his bed and get home.

A tear fell onto her cheek when she thought about how she had asked him angrily why he was so damned determined to get home. To which he responded that it was the first of the month, and he needed to get his disability check out of his mailbox. She recalled asking why he couldn't just call a family member to pick up his stupid check.

A pang in her stomach arose as she could almost hear him grunt words to the effect that *I ain't got nobody to do that, and I'm the only one who should do it. They gon' steal my check. If I don't have my money, I can't pay my rent. And I don't wanna end up in a shelter again. And who gon' pay for my food and my medicines?*

Her tears slipped down her cheeks like large water drops landing on an oiled slide onto her gown. The drops started to free fall as she recalled saying to Chester, in essence, *I don't care* and *get back in bed.* She thought about the fact that she had no real concern about his lot in life because she'd only been focused on herself. She remembered that a couple of days after her encounter with Chester, a social worker employed by the hospital informed her that his social security check had been stolen from his mailbox while he was in Grady and the social services department was trying to figure out how to assist him.

At that time, Grace was slightly sympathetic to his situation but certainly had no real empathy for him. She had assumed that Chester was the classic example of a person satisfied with simply existing and didn't try hard enough in his formative years to make something of his life.

Chester's anger, commixed with depression, appeared to overpower his ability to communicate with her after that event. Near the end of that hospitalization, he broke his silence by initially answering asked questions about how he felt physically during morning rounds.

But his bottled-up words erupted from his mouth like lava spewing from a dormant volcano one morning as he quickly countered her questions with answers. As if out of nowhere, he spewed that he didn't like her and that he felt she treated him with disrespect. He had gone on the say that people like her always thought they were better than everybody else and that's why he didn't like dealing with doctors who had their noses in the air. He told her that she never really looked at his face when she asked him how he was doing. She was always looking at a clipboard or paying attention to what was on the television in his room. He'd told her that high-classed people like her were no better than him.

At that time, she refused to receive his criticisms. As a practicing physician, she occasionally used patients like Chester as an example of the noncompliant patient and how they added an extra burden on their recovery and the overall healthcare system.

She had never cried when thinking or talking about him before. But his words pierced her now. Sitting in the bed, trembling despite the warmth in the room, she felt as though she entered Chester's pain for the first time. Chester also had been one of her teachers and she hadn't passed that test. He had offered her tutoring in respect for her fellow man, silencing judgements, and appreciating likenesses rather than focusing on minor differences.

"Health and death equalize us all," she whispered softly.

When Grace thought about her well-educated father's battle with diabetes and renal failure even before the cancer diagnosis, she realized that he and Chester weren't all that different. Remembering her dad's medical noncompliance and anger about his failing health was like seeing a photo with split images. Although her dad had a Doctor of Theology degree, he didn't believe in the healthcare system and medical doctors. She'd once even told him that his dichotomy was hypocritical, especially since he had encouraged her to become a physician. But she witnessed a strong, proud man, who initially refused to believe his test results were correct when he was told he had diabetes, wither from the disease. He struggled with having to take insulin. But, like Chester, depression set in when it seemed her father's condition was too far gone and no longer manageable.

She felt terrible and so wanted to change her thought processes. She took a deep breath and thought about calling Stewart, but texted instead.

All is well. I'll call you in the morning. Thanks for loving me.

Stewart then replied.

Okay. I can't help but love you. I hope things have gone well. I'll be up early so call when u can.

CHAPTER 31

G race tapped the radio icon on her cell phone. She chose a spa station in an attempt to create an atmosphere of relaxation and absorb her thoughts about Chester and her dad. The serene sounds of ocean waves rushed towards a shore and the ebbing harmonious retreat of the waters tried to still her spirit. She drifted in and out of rest as she attempted to ditch her anxiety and regret.

She lay back on the bed, floating above ocean sounds and willing her thoughts to her chance meeting with Stewart nearly fifteen years before. That memory always made her feel better.

Nearing sleep, she wandered back in time to a cold, gray January morning after a long night on call as a gastroenterology fellow at Emory Hospital. She was standing at the gas station and her gas cap wouldn't turn, either due to the cold or her lack of strength. She envisioned Stewart watching her. Stewart, a gorgeous young man with a beautiful smile, came over and offered to help. She waved her hand as she was drifting off to sleep, motioning him to go away as she tried to get back in her car, embarrassed about her unkempt post-call appearance. But a red warning low fuel signal flashing in the car console forced her to accept his offer.

The mellow echoes of Stewart's voice mixed with the waves from the radio as he introduced himself while popping off the gas cap. Her weak *thank you* and his response about *ladies in distress* brought her comfort. In her dream state, Stewart breathed clouds of air that condensed with every word from his mouth.

As he proceeded to pump her gas, he talked about how unusually cold the weather was in Atlanta that year. She saw a vision of herself walking away from him with her index finger raised like every good Baptist should do as the proper way to excuse herself. She disappeared to pay for her gas.

She fantasized about how he looked when she returned, leaning sexily against her car as he asked her if she'd worked all night. Eyeing his well-chiseled face in a cluster of dream clouds, she felt a soft warmth. She accepted his business card. He asked for her information and if he could call her someday soon. The morning of their chance introduction folded into their goodbye. She saw herself lying on top of a pile of clothes that covered her bed in her disorganized Atlanta apartment. She could hear a phone ring that seemed very real, so she opened her eyes to check her cell. There was no call. She realized she had been dreaming and willed herself back to sleep, hoping to pick up where she left off because it was such a pleasant dream.

Becoming aware of the radio again, she heard a light flute playing a mediation song that sounded like she was in an Asian Zen Buddhist temple. As she listened, she drifted back into her dream. She heard Stewart's deep, inviting voice asking her something about getting much-needed rest and not needing to drive, given the state she was in. She was back to the first few days of their meeting. Grace floated in her dream state as she could hear him say that he was the guy from the gas station and his name was Stewart Livingston.

You looked exhausted, she heard Stewart's velvet voice echo.

Through the murky scene of them talking and him asking her out for dinner that evening, she began to breathe heavily and snore softly.

The blaring of fog horns signaled her phone's alarm. She slammed her hand aimlessly to find it and silenced the alarm. She pulled the phone to her face and focused to see that it was 6:30 a.m. She was anxious about the day ahead, so she sat on the side of the bed but quickly realized she needed a few minutes to get her bearings. After ten minutes or so had passed, her brain fog dissipated. The dream of Stewart came to mind and she smiled.

Grace got up from the bed, entered the bathroom, and sat at the vanity. She unloaded items from her travel kit, including her curling iron, makeup bag, perfume, lotion, and deodorant. She plugged the curling iron into the bathroom socket and turned it to its highest setting. She covered her mouth and muffled a cough. She smiled as she looked at her curling iron and thought about her first date with Stewart.

On the night of the date, she'd grabbed five different outfits to try on. She finally settled on a lime green wool blazer with a tan silk tank top and tan silk slacks that accentuated her figure. She had a photo from that night in their family room in Knoxville as her constant reminder. Grace remembered having washed and blow-dried her hair hurriedly that night and then heating up her curling iron much like she was doing now.

But on the evening of her date with Stewart, as she was in the process of curling her last lock of hair, the curling iron slipped out of her hand and fell onto the bridge of her nose, causing a scalding burn. She lost most of the skin on the lower third of her nose. She thought about how that night appeared to be headed for disaster.

Grace recalled her embarrassment when he arrived and she answered the door with her hand over her nose, telling him that she had experienced a small accident. She remembered his look of disappointment when she told him that she couldn't go out to eat. "I'm so sorry," she'd said.

As he lowered her hand from her nose, he had asked, "What could be so wrong?"

She thought that this man was definitely meant for her. Who would have thought that such a gorgeous man, who had seen her looking like a fright at a gas station and again for their *first* date, would stick around? She remembered his laughter as he told her that she looked great. He had offered to pick up something for them to eat at her house.

A seemingly bad situation allowed them to get to know each other better that night with few interruptions, except for the times that he acted like he was the doctor, nursing her nose.

Grace heard Hanna and Glen stirring around in the hallway. She knew she needed to hurry but was caught up in her thoughts. As she sat at the mirror and began putting on her makeup, attempting to cover the dark circles under her eyes, she continued to think about her first date with Stewart.

Stewart was in his take-charge mode that night and appeared to be relaxed in her home. With ease, he opened kitchen cabinets, put dishes on the table, opened the cute white boxed containers dishing lo mien, cashew chicken, and egg rolls onto their plates. He'd said, *Come over here to the table and let me serve you.*

She never forgot those words because no man had ever said them to her before. He poured glasses of white zinfandel and then asked her about candles. Grace smiled as she remembered his response to the look on her face, *Oops, bad suggestion. I guess we don't need candles, do we? One of us may start a fire and we don't want the Atlanta Fire Department over here.*

They decided there had been enough burns for the day. So, no candles. They'd cracked open their fortune cookies and she fondly remembered Stewart saying that his said love was in the air. She teased him about having paid someone to stow that fortune in the bag. She smiled, remembering the warmth of Stewart's arm as he placed it around her shoulders when they sat near each other on the sofa, and he whispered softly about how cute her nose looked. She recalled offering him the sofa for the night and him falling asleep like a rock in a matter of minutes. On that night, she decided that Stewart was her destined soul mate.

CHAPTER 32

"Grace, are you ready to go?" Hanna asked as she knocked on the door.

"Not quite. Sorry, I'm moving a little slow but I'll be right out."

Grace hurriedly put on her black jeans, white tank, and black jacket. She quickly put her toiletries and clothes away after making up the bed. As she came out of the room, she smiled at Hanna and said, "Good morning, I am a snail this morning. Sorry for the delay. I didn't sleep as well as I had hoped, I guess."

She and Hanna walked out to Hanna's car and started their drive.

"So, why couldn't you sleep?" Hanna asked.

"I'm not sure. It wasn't the bed because it was quite comfortable. I've just been on a road of remembrance or something. Even when I think I'm resting, my thoughts are racing. It was a little cool in my room last night, too. Maybe I couldn't sleep because of that," she said in jest, hoping to change the subject.

"Grace, why didn't you just come and tell me? You know I would've turned up the heat."

"I know. I'm sorry. Your home is wonderful and there is not a thing wrong with your hospitality," Grace replied.

"Hey, you know I can tell when you are trying to throw up a smoke screen, right?"

"Am I that obvious?"

"You've had to absorb a lot of stuff in a fairly short period of time. I've been your sister long enough to know that you're not accustomed to having the reins taken out of your hands. This has to be eating you alive."

Grace turned away and quietly looked out of the window.

"Oh, God, I'm so sorry for saying that, Grace. Could I have been more insensitive?"

"No, it's all good. The fact of the matter is that cancer does eat away at the body," responded Grace.

"I'm so sorry," Hanna said empathetically.

"If only I had seen this coming, I could have mapped out a plan about how I wanted all of this to go. I wouldn't have taken the new position at my job and would have spent more time preparing the kids for what to expect. Oh hell, I would have just spent more time with my family."

"Hey, listen. We don't have crystal balls stuck in our foreheads and we aren't clairvoyant. Stop beating yourself up. Your kids will be fine. Children are far more resilient than us old farts."

Grace didn't respond as she looked at the rows of trees sweeping past her dizzied eyes.

"Plus, I remember Daddy saying once or twice that when we stop trying to fix our issues, God fixes them for us. We just mess things up trying to work them out by ourselves."

A couple of minutes later, Grace said wearily, "I know you're probably right. It's just that I have a lot going on in my head."

Hanna pushed the radio icon on her dashboard, selected CD player, and pressed selection three, *The Best of Stevie Wonder*. Grace refocused on the trees while listening to Stevie singing, *don't you worry 'bout a thing*. Hanna reached over and squeezed Grace's hand.

CHAPTER 33

As they were making their way to Tracewoods Drive, Hanna asked Grace, "Have you thought about how you want to start the conversation?"

"I was thinking about possibly asking Naomi to pray a family prayer? Then maybe start by telling them about my fall first," said Grace.

"Well, you really want them to be suspect, don't you?"

"Why would you say that?" asked Grace.

"I don't think you have ever asked anyone to pray for you other than Mama or Daddy."

"I don't think that's true, but anyway, I need some of Naomi's faith right about now."

"Not to throw a wrench in the conversation, but you know none of us have really been willing to make a final decision on Dad and Mom's property. Maybe I can lead off the morning with that if you're hesitant about discussing the cancer right off the bat," Hanna suggested.

Grace pondered that.

"I want to sell it now, and I think Sam does, too, in all honesty. I know that Naomi and Sara are not quite there yet, but with you facing this health crisis and none of us getting any younger, we need to tie up this loose end. What do you think, Grace?"

"It's probably not a bad time to revisit the selling prospect," Grace replied. "But that place has so much history wrapped up in it. I can see why it's hard for Naomi and Sara to say goodbye."

"I know, but I think this is a good time to at least approach the issue."

"Okay, if you want to bring it up, I'll be happy to discuss it. But the decision has to be unanimous," said Grace.

As they pulled into the driveway, Hanna said, "Okay, but I will say that, as cold as it is this morning, I'm glad we kept the utilities on over here."

Grace noticed that Samuel's car was already in the driveway. Hanna laughed as she said, "Oh, let me guess—Mr. Protector is already here making sure the house is warm enough. I'll bet he's been here an hour already. He is so much like Daddy, it's not even funny."

Grace smiled and joined in with a weak laugh. "You're probably right."

When they opened the door, they smelled coffee brewing. Samuel had also brought baked goods along with his coffee pot from his house.

"Hey, ladies, I brought Grace lots of fattening treats. We've got to put some meat on her bones."

"Wait a second, you didn't say that about me. So, I'm not gonna get anything to eat because I'm too chunky?" Hanna accused.

"Oh, please, Hanna, you look fine. But I have enough pastries here to feed a small village."

Sara and Naomi arrived about twenty minutes later. Naomi came through the door singing, "This is the day that the Lord has made, let us rejoice and be glad in it."

"You're the only one who needs to be pumped up this morning, so hush up. We're all just fine and don't need a sermon on Saturday morning," said Hanna.

Grace managed to laugh and thought Hanna needed to speak for herself.

"I still love coming over here," Sara said. "Grace, thanks for suggesting that we meet here. Even though I'm right here in town, I don't get by enough."

"Agreed," said Hanna.

Grace sensed that Hanna might use this as her opening. So, she turned to Hanna and said, "Guys, Hanna wants to discuss the sale of the house in the near future, before I get started."

"Is this why you asked us to come over here?" asked Naomi.

"No, it's not, but I told Grace this might be a good time to discuss this subject again," Hanna replied.

"Hanna, you can't push us to sell this place!" exclaimed Naomi.

"I don't want to argue about this, but Grace and I are often left paying most of the expenses over here, and you guys know that."

Grace chimed in with tearing eyes, "This is not how I wanted today to go. Hanna, can we just let that subject rest right now?"

"Are you okay, Grace?" asked Sara.

"Don't y'all miss our Thanksgivings and Christmas holidays that we enjoyed as kids here when Mama sang *We gather to together to ask the Lord's blessings* while cooking her creamy dressing and her flawless golden-brown turkey? This is a truly nostalgic place for me," said Grace through sniffles.

Naomi picked up a pastry from the kitchen counter and poured a cup of steaming black coffee. After taking a large bite of her Danish and a large gulp of coffee that appeared to scald her mouth, Naomi asked, "Grace, why did we have to come over so early this morning? Why didn't you say what you had to say last night?"

Sara wiped crumbs from her mouth. "Stop it, Naomi. Grace is clearly emotional right now. So, go on, Grace. What's your big announcement? Naomi and I made a bet about what you're going to say. I guessed you're going to tell us you got some crazy promotion that's going to take you to Africa or somewhere. And Naomi thinks you're going to be president of the medical school. So, which is it?"

Sara stopped mid-smile when she saw the distressed look on Grace's face. Sara tossed the remainder of her pastry into the garbage can and poured out her coffee.

"Let's all go into the den and find a seat wherever we can," said Hanna.

Naomi and Hanna picked up another pastry and sat on the fireplace ledge.

Grace hesitated, then walked into the den and sat on the corner section of the plaid sofa. Her top lip began to quiver. Samuel came to her side, sitting on the arm of the couch. Sara sat on the other side of her.

Grace panned the room, then looked up at Samuel. "Um, I recently found out that I have advanced breast cancer. And my doctor has told me that I'll need to have a mastectomy soon and have to start chemotherapy."

Silence filled the room for a few seconds, but it felt like an eternity to Grace. Naomi stood up. "Jesus, Jesus, Jesus."

Sara, who was always the quiet one in the family, rubbed her sister's back and began to cry. "Oh, my God, this is certainly not at all what I was expecting," she said through tears.

Grace laid her head on Sara's shoulder and looked off into space for a few seconds. "I was thrown for a loop, too. You guys know how I am. I just didn't see this coming!"

Naomi was the first to ask, "How advanced is this cancer? What does it mean that you need both a mastectomy and chemotherapy? Do you know what stage it's in?"

"They won't know everything until I have surgery, but the grade of the cancer is not good. I was surprised when I found the lump in my breast. I had fallen at work a few days before I found it and thought I just had a blood clot that wouldn't go away."

There was silence in the room again. Although she was the one with cancer, she felt the need to comfort her family. Sitting in their parents' home, she imagined that all kinds of memories had to be flooding their minds. She thought that maybe they were envisioning the worst possible outcome.

"As I said," Grace continued, "my pathology was somewhat worrisome, according to my doctor. But she's hopeful. My doctor happens to be Shelley, whom you guys know. She thinks that I might need radiation, as well. But, again, Shelley won't know the final details until after I've had the surgery which is scheduled for Friday."

"Wow," said Naomi. "We need to pray right now, y'all."

"I was hoping you would say that. I've been wondering if God is trying to test me. Do you know what I mean?" asked Grace.

"God is not like that, Grace. He wants what's best for us. Now, I know I can't spin a cancer diagnosis into something positive. But I believe God will show you in time what this all means."

"Well, I'm open to hearing whatever He has to say," responded Grace.

Naomi walked over and grabbed Grace's hand. "Let's all stand in a circle and hold hands. We need to pray right now."

They all rose. Grace looked at Naomi and smiled as she sensed their father's pastoral tone in Naomi's voice and thought that her mom was right about Naomi having hidden gifts.

Naomi began to pray, her voice flowing and crescendoing, "Dear Heavenly Father, we, your children, bow our heads in humble submission to you. Lord, we're shocked and weren't expecting to hear this sad news about our precious sister. She needs You now to give her direction and yes, Lord, she needs a healing. We know You already know her destiny, but we're asking You for a miracle as only You can do. Grace is frightened and so are we but you are the ultimate comforter. Please, undergird her faith and give her what she needs. Even if the doctors have told her that the cancer is advanced, You are the Master Physician who can do all things and turn it around. And Lord, help us to be the support that she will need. Keep us strong for her."

Naomi's voice broke as she continued, "But not our will, but Thy will be done. Amen."

Naomi hugged Grace in a tight embrace. As they swayed back and forth, Grace felt an emotional cleansing overwhelming her. Grace's shoulders jerked as she sobbed in Naomi's arms. Hanna walked over and placed her hand on Grace's back along with Sara. Samuel sat back on the edge of the sofa and quietly looked down at the floor.

Grace sniffled as she walked back over to the sofa, sat down, and placed her hand on Samuel's knee.

"Coming home has always helped me. This time, I believe God has brought back some memories that have both challenged me and brought me peace. I'm gonna be fine."

"How long have you known?" asked Naomi.

"It's only been a few days. But, like I said, I actually came home to clear my head and tell you guys face to face. I didn't want to do this over the phone."

Hanna began to cry, "This just isn't fair."

Grace knew from past experiences that Hanna had a tendency to go to dark places because of her own history.

Hanna asked, "Does God really care about this family?"

"That's ridiculous, Hanna, please, don't go there!" Sara retorted

Grace was a little surprised by Hanna's outburst, but knew that she suffered emotional scars from her first marriage in that she had experienced domestic abuse at the hand of her first husband, Quinton, while she was living in Los Angeles. He had beaten her many times before she shared her problems with the family. Their parents were still alive at that time and their dad had been there to counsel her through the ordeal. Their mom had been so horrified that one of her children had gone through such brutal attacks that she required anxiety medication for a short time. Hanna had been hospitalized at least twice due to the offenses. Hanna forgave Quinton initially but saw that the chain of dysfunction was moving towards her children. So, she found a way out. Her divorce was marked by threats on her life and the lives of their kids. While Quinton was incarcerated for making the threats, Hanna moved back to Mississippi to be near her family.

"Hanna, I hear you. I have done some soul-searching myself and asked why. But you know, now I don't believe God has turned His back on me or any of us for that matter. Remember, you encouraged me earlier and told me that your faith had strengthened over the past few years. Don't let my diagnosis set you back. I believe things happen for a reason. Though this is a challenging time for me, I'm at least talking more with God and focusing on the things that matter most in my life right now. In all honesty, I don't think I have ever taken the time to reflect about my life's journey the way I have done in this past week. I have been so driven to do the next great thing that I've rarely focused on my here and now. In some ways, Stewart and my kids have been the casualties of my success."

Grace smiled faintly as she went on to say, "I remember hearing Daddy say once, "I wouldn't take nothing for my journey now," as he was coming to the end of his life. I think I understand what he meant. It's amazing. I have had so many wonderful things happen in my life but when I look back at what God has brought me through, I am amazed at His wondrous kindness in it all. Now, mind you, I am not planning on dying anytime soon, but this disease has caused me to pause."

"Are you trying to put up a front for us, Grace? Remember, we have been together forever and know each other," said Sara.

"No, I'll admit that I'm afraid. But, really, being home with you all and just getting it out has lifted a heavy weight off my chest. You guys have always thought I was the strong one but I'm going to need your help in the coming months. I'm not asking you to drop everything and move to Tennessee. But I'll need to hear your voices as much as possible and of course, we will video chat like crazy." She turned to Samuel and squeezed his hand.

"I'm not sure I'm going to be able to come to the wedding, though. But I'm going to try my hardest to be there."

"Baby sis, that is the least of my concerns. You focus on your health and beating this thing. And I mean that," Samuel said with the deepest sincerity.

She reminded him that family is always there for each other. They all sat for a while in quiet and looked around the room.

Sara broke the silence. "Girl, we are going to have to get you a slamming wig. The Wilson girls have always been known for being well dressed and having their 'do' put together nice."

Naomi and Hanna nodded as they forced a smile.

"Grace, we'll certainly make sure that you are the best-looking cancer patient around. But seriously, we're going to make sure you are taken care of," said Hanna.

"What are your plans for work, and how are Stewart and the kids handling all of this?" asked Naomi.

"Stewart has been amazing. He's trying to decide if we should have Alice move in for a while when I get started with the chemotherapy, depending on how it affects me. God knows, I realize how blessed I am. There are so many women who face this same struggle or worse, and don't have the resources I have available to me."

"Good to know that Stewart is being so supportive," said Sara.

"Yeah, he really is. I've been feeling sorry for myself, but I know that I'm fortunate to have a great husband and family. I've had patients with cancer who didn't even know if they could afford the treatments or even have the means to make it to their treatments. And there is nothing sadder than a person who has no family support whatsoever."

"Wow, I never thought about it that way," said Naomi as she shook her head.

"As for work, that's going to be tricky because I actually did get a promotion of sorts there. Dr. Malloy had just named me the new director of the fellowship program right before I found out about the cancer. I've made him aware of everything going on with me. He knows I'll be out for a few weeks. I'm not sure he'll be able to hold that position for me because the department has to move forward with or without me. I'm actually okay with whatever they decide."

"How have the kids been doing since you told them?" asked Sara.

"We haven't told the kids yet. That's going to be hard for me," said Grace.

"You're going to tell them soon though, right?" asked Sara.

"I will, but to tell you the truth, Patrice already senses something is wrong. She has been more attentive to me since the day Shelley told Stewart and me about the biopsy results. For the last few days, she's been the polar opposite of the child I've complained to you guys about for this past year. And, well, Christopher is my baby, and I worry most about him. Right now, his world revolves around soccer, video games, and his telescope, which is how it should be. My worry is that this could turn his life upside down. Stewart and I are going to have the big discussion with them when I get back to Knoxville."

Samuel stood up. "Hey, I can take off as much time as I need to from work and be there with you and the kids. I've accumulated tons of vacation and sick days."

"Thanks, Sam, but save your time for your newlywed days. The love I feel in this room is enough to carry me through whatever is to come. You know, I feel as if Daddy and Mama are here with us right now, too."

"Is anyone still hungry? If you are, grab a pastry because I'm going to clean up the kitchen," said Sara from across the room.

Naomi and Hanna joined her in cleaning up. Hanna nibbled on a leftover pastry as she whispered, "What do you guys think about me asking Clara if she can work us in at her spa today? Or do you think that would be a bit awkward?"

"Actually, I think it's just what Grace needs to get her mind off things. We should try to do it if she can accommodate us. I'm supposed to have a hair appointment at her place today anyway," said Sara.

"Okay, let me call and see what she can work out," said Hanna.

Grace met Sara's glance as she looked back into the den while stuffing empty Styrofoam cups into a white trash bag.

Sara stepped back into the room and asked, "Grace, do you have any other plans for the day?"

"No, I didn't sleep well last night, so a nap is my only real agenda item."

Samuel moved closer to Grace and said, "I liked your strong lady speech, but I'm concerned about you. Listen, can we go out to dinner later this evening so that we can really have a heart to heart talk?"

"Samuel, I'm okay, now. I was making myself more anxious just trying to second-guess how you guys were going to react. I needed to get it out. Like I said earlier, I didn't want to do this over the phone. Instead of dinner, let's plan on a walk or something later today and we can talk then."

"All right, I guess that'll have to do," said Samuel.

Hanna came back into the room and said, "Grace, Naomi just asked me a good question. How is it that your mammogram missed the tumor? I thought that was why we get those—to diagnose cancer."

"I don't know and neither does my oncologist. Shelley quoted some statistics about how often mammograms miss tumors and reminded me that it's not a 100% predictive test."

"Well, should we all have our mammograms redone?" asked Hanna.

"No, I don't think that's necessary but it's your choice. I found the lump in my breast while showering. You all may want to do manual exams on yourselves every month, though breast self-exam is not recommended like it used to be by physicians. By the way, Sara, did you have your colonoscopy like I asked you to do? I'm sorry, it's hard for me not be a doctor."

Sara quirked a brow and said, "I should have known you would find a way to sneak that one in. I've been procrastinating but I'm going to call my doctor's office on Monday. I promise."

"I would appreciate that. I don't need to worry about you too."

"I promise."

CHAPTER 34

They closed up the house after the kitchen had been cleaned to Hanna's satisfaction. Naomi and Sara, who had ridden together, mentioned that they had to run some errands. Samuel hugged everyone and drove away. Grace and Hanna journeyed back to Hanna's house and talked more on their ride.

"I'm actually glad we had the house to go to today for you to share your diagnosis. I know now why you wanted to be there. I felt Daddy and Mama's spirit today, too. We've seen a lot as family on Tracewoods Drive, haven't we?" said Hanna.

"Yes, we have," answered Grace.

As Hanna was about to turned into her driveway, she stopped and said, "I know this must be hard for you, but you're not alone. I'm going to be with you as much as I can. I'm not just saying that either."

"I've never questioned your love and I know that I have one of the best families on earth. I don't take it for granted. Again, thanks for allowing me to stay on such short notice."

"Oh, please! That's what family is all about."

After they arrived back at the house, Grace went upstairs to the guest room and lay across the bed. She had plans to return home early Sunday morning, but decided she would probably leave after church on Sunday or maybe even early Monday. She liked what she felt at the altar at Second Baptist and wanted to spend a little more time at the church and with her siblings. She rolled over and grabbed her phone from her purse. She called Stewart but there was no answer. It immediately went to his voicemail twice. She clutched her phone to her chest because she was so hoping to hear his voice. She figured he had probably taken the kids to the skating rink or was doing work from his phone.

After two more unsuccessful attempts, she left him a voicemail saying, "Things went well. Call me later. Oh, yes, I'll probably leave later tomorrow or Monday morning. I can't wait to see you all. I miss you so much. Love you."

Grace laid her phone on the bedside table and connected it to a power cord. She sighed as she finally felt some degree of relaxation. She surmised that she had worked herself into a nervous frenzy over just telling them. Why do I do that to myself? she thought. She could hear Stewart saying, "You've got to stop trying to manage everybody's emotions." *That's definitely something I need to work on.*

She coughed, took a deep breath, and dozed off to sleep while replaying Naomi's prayer in her mind and thinking of how much Naomi had grown. She had been sleeping for about an hour or so when she heard a soft knock on the door. It was Sara, who asked, "Are you asleep? Can I come in?"

Grace rolled over, let out a deep cough, and looked at the ceiling for a second as she tried to get her bearings. "I was just resting a bit, but sure, you can come in."

"Great," said Sara.

"What are you doing here? I thought you and Naomi had some errands to run."

"We did a couple of things but we're done now. Can you come downstairs so that we can all talk?"

Oh no, more questions. I thought they were okay with our discussion this morning? Oh, well, this is why I came, so let's just do it.

To Grace's surprise, when she came downstairs, her sisters yelled in unison, "Emergency sister therapy!"

Grace smiled and rolled her eyes because she was the one who invented *the emergency therapy plan.*

"A therapy session, huh?" Grace said through a smile.

The last time they had one of those, they had eaten so much that no one was able to move from the table when the waiter said that the restaurant was about to close.

"I called Clara and she put us down today for spa treatments at her new salon and spa. I had to play my best friend card to get us all worked in for services. She has asked that we come through the back door though, so that her other customers don't get angry. We can each have either a facial or a massage along with a manicure or pedicure. Her nieces are going to come in today and help us out."

"It's just after noon on a Saturday, surely she was already fully booked," said Grace.

"Don't be mad at me, but I told her about what's going on with you, and since Clara has known us most of our lives, she was honored to be able to do something for you," said Hanna.

Sitting with wide eyes, Grace was about to ask Hanna why she had told someone about her illness without her permission, but she decided to stifle her response. She took a deep breath and asked herself if it was her pride or not wanting to be pitied that was her real concern here. Either way, it made her uncomfortable. But her thoughts went back to Stewart telling her that she doesn't have to be superwoman and that she needed to let go. She forced a smile and said, "Well, what are we waiting for? Let's get the party started. Feels like old times."

CHAPTER 35

They arrived at the spa and were escorted from the back door to a changing room. They each got undressed and put on soft, white terry cloth robes with the initials CDS (Clara's Day Spa) written over the left breast pocket. They were taken to a quiet room where Grace noticed a plate of fresh cut fruit, yogurt parfaits, and mixed nuts waiting for them along with sparkling cider. Sara poured each of them a glass of cider into chilled champagne flutes.

"You guys work fast. How did you plan this on such short notice?" Grace asked Hanna.

"Actually, Naomi and I stopped and picked up the fruit tray, cider, and parfaits. The mixed nuts are Clara's usual treats for her guests. We brought everything over once Hanna told us we had a green light to come over here. Plus, we had already planned an apple cider toast in response to what we thought was going to be your great news," said Sara.

Instead, they toasted to Grace's protection through surgery and full recovery.

"Grace, what's your real concern about telling the kids?" Sara asked. "You and I both know they can handle this."

"I just want them to stay focused on their school work right now as long as they can. Plus, since I was coming to

Mississippi, I didn't want Stewart to be left behind with lots of questions for him to have to answer alone."

"Is that all?" asked Sara.

"Not really. I've been in a dream state of sorts for the past several days. Once I tell them, this becomes more real, if that makes any sense. I'm not ready to have to answer their questions. I know that sounds selfish. But, I'm not sure I'm strong enough. I'm their mom, their protector, and I feel so defeated right now."

"Grace, as I told you before, children are much more resilient than we are. I think they're going to surprise you. Plus, you can rest assured that they'll be tougher than me," said Hanna.

"Anyway, Miss Smarty Pants' Patrice will probably have the surgical procedure and any other treatments you might need researched before the oncologist can tell you what's going to actually happen," said Naomi.

Grace nodded. "Can't you just see Patrice calling Auntie Shelley and saying so—*Tell me exactly how do you plan to treat my mother.*"

They all laughed because they knew she was absolutely right.

"Patrice and I are connected, but Christopher is definitely a mama's boy. What is my sweet boy going to do?" asked Grace.

"Grace, you and Stewart have done a great job raising those children and they are going to be just fine," said Naomi.

They all chimed in together and reminded her that they would be there for the kids, too. They would be checking in on the children as often as they could.

Clara stepped into the quiet room and asked Grace if she was ready for her massage. Three other therapists entered after her and called each of the sisters back. Clara hugged Grace and said, "I'm so sorry to hear about what's been going on, girl. I just hate that. But Hanna really wants you to have a good time today so you can take your mind off of things."

"Thanks for your concern. I haven't told a lot of people yet. Hanna gets carried away sometimes. But I do appreciate you doing this for us."

"I feel like I was practically raised by your parents because they were such a central part of my life growing up. Y'alls family seemed like the perfect family, like y'all didn't have no problems. I think that's why I was so drawn to Hanna as a friend. Your mom checked on my homework more than my mom did. Not having a father at home, Pastor Wilson seemed to always be there for me and my brother. So, we're family, honey. Let me pamper you. Plus, I rarely get to see you anymore," said Clara.

"You're sweet for saying such kind words. Clara, if you don't mind, I don't want to talk a lot right now. Also, I have a habit of falling asleep during massages," said Grace.

"This is your day. If you want to sleep, so be it. Your wish is my command, sweetie."

Grace took off her robe and climbed onto the massage table, face down. Sounds of soothing music increased around her as her musles began to relax. Clara began kneading her shoulders and back. As the massage seemed to be increasing blood flow to her fingers, she realized that she did need some emergency sister therapy. At some point during her massage, she fell asleep.

While asleep, Grace's memories of her time at Emory Hospital returned. She was in the ICU this time with a couple from Macon, Georgia. The patient, Mr. Peters, had been incorrectly diagnosed with leukemia by his local oncologist and had been treated for months without success. Grace saw a shadowy figure of a large-framed man writhing in pain. She could hear the billowy sounds of his wife saying, *Walter is a wonderful husband and father and prides himself on being the main breadwinner for our family. But, Lord, he looks so helpless in that hospital bed. I'm just praying I get my husband back home, whole and healthy.* But Grace saw that shadowy figure dwindling away as his misdiagnosed leukemia was revealed to be multiple myeloma. Mr. Peters never responded to aggressive chemotherapy as his disease had progressed to a point of no return and he ultimately died.

Grace could almost feel his family's deep mourning as cries, screams, and scenes of running in disbelief tossed around in her brain. Their hero and giant of a husband and father had died. Grace stirred on the massage table as she heard a nurse say, "Those people should be ashamed of themselves for carrying on like fools. What's with all the drama?"

Mr. Peters' face melted into her father's face in her dream. When she looked up at her father who was standing over her, he grabbed her tear-covered hands. He said, "As pastors, we often focus on the family of the deceased, but rarely think about the effect death has on the professional caregivers." Her father was praying for her in her dream and she cried all the more.

Grace felt a quake. Clara was shaking her and asking, "Are you all right? You fell asleep for a while but then started shouting and crying. Were you having a bad dream? I'm so sorry that you're having to go through this. Lord, baby, you gon' be all right."

"I'm fine. You're right. I must have been dreaming. I'm sorry if I frightened you. I probably need to go back to Hanna's house. Clara, thanks for everything."

"Wait, you still have some time left on your massage. I was just about to have you turn over," encouraged Clara.

"I appreciate everything but I need to go. Sorry for interrupting your day this way, Clara," said Grace.

"Okay," said Clara as she left the room.

Grace put her robe back on and went back to the quiet room. Upon Grace's entrance, she noticed that Sara was there.

"I thought you were getting a message, Sara?" questioned Grace.

"I opted for a mini-massage so that I could still get my hair done. Are you okay? Your eyes are red!"

Grace answered, "I'm fine. I fell asleep and woke up from a crazy dream that I guess caused me to cry, and I scared poor Clara. I was dreaming about a patient I saw years ago who had a misdiagnosed cancer. I don't know, maybe his misdiagnosis and my missed tumor brought that patient back to me. He died and then I saw Daddy and I guess it was just too much for my subconscious. I'm good, though."

"Grace, it's okay if you're afraid. Do you feel comfortable with all of your doctors?"

"Shelley's handling all that for me. Actually, I know my surgeon and he's the best in the city. If I need radiation, Shelley will help me choose the radiation oncologist, too. Although she is my physician, she is going to act as a health coordinator of sorts for me. She asked Dr. Grier to be my primary oncologist because she feels she's too close to me. She's going to be a part of my care team, though. I think this whole thing has gotten Shelley worked up, too, because she thought the lump was going to be nothing just like I did."

"I'm happy you have Shelley to lean on there. But can you be sure we all have Shelley's contact information, including her cell phone number, before you go back home?"

"Sure. I'll need to check with her, but I suspect it won't be a problem. No matter what, you'll be able to talk with Stewart. But you know, Sara, being the patient is going to be very weird for me. I've got to learn to let go. Or at least, I need to give it my level best to try to do so. You know me— once a control freak, always a control freak. I'm usually the one giving the orders and telling patients what to expect. But now I've got to trust my care to someone else."

Sara smirked. "I wouldn't call you a control freak. I think world champion micromanager is more appropriate."

They both laughed.

After Sara left the quiet room, Grace leaned back on the chaise lounge as she waited for Hanna. As the room became quiet again, she remembered visiting her mother in her dying days. Grace had been so frustrated with the fact that every medical intervention offered to help her mom seemed to make her worse. She realized that despite all of her medical knowledge, she couldn't do anything for her dear mama to turn her circumstances around. Grace contemplated the guilt she carried for a while because of that. She had worn her medical badge of honor across her chest proudly for years so that the world could see that she was in the business of healing people, but she couldn't help her mother.

After their massages and other treatments, the sisters dressed in the dressing room. Clara came back to the quiet room, hugged Grace, and said, "Are better now? Please know that you're in my prayers."

Grace thanked her. "Clara, you're a jewel and I'll be just fine. I sure hope my sister has paid you for all of this because I know you've lost some money having to fit us in."

"I wouldn't have it any other way. Besides, I am a full-figured girl who likes to eat. Hanna usually treats me and my staff well by bringing a feast to eat from time to time on our busiest days. It all works out. I'm just so happy to see you, Grace."

Sara popped out from behind a curtain. "I decided to just get my hair pulled back in a quick French roll so that I'd be able to leave with everyone. Ready to go?"

They each hugged Clara and said their goodbyes. Then the sisters headed back to Hanna's.

CHAPTER 36

As they pulled into the driveway, and were laughing about Naomi's crazy purple nail color selection, Grace said, "Are you about to show us your wild side now, baby sister?"

Naomi giggled, "You know it."

As their car doors opened, Grace squinted as she focused on Hanna's front door. She saw Patrice and Chris run out to hug her. Samuel was standing on the sidewalk and Stewart stood in the doorway, looking at her with a smile. Grace began to cry.

She hugged each child as tightly as she could, causing Chris to say, "Mom, I'm not a baby anymore. This is a little embarrassing."

Patrice rolled her eyes. "Oh, please! Mom, he was the main one whining about wanting to see his mommy. He kept asking what was taking us so long to get here. *I miss Mommy*, he kept saying."

Grace let go of him. "No problem, guys. I missed you all, too. Chris, like it or not, you will always be my baby."

She pinched his cheeks and patted him on his head.

The children ran to their aunts and gave them hugs, as well. Stewart was still standing in the doorway when Grace walked over to him getting a hug and kiss.

"So, you got me. I didn't expect this," said Grace.

"I still have a few tricks up my sleeve, Dr. Livingston," said Stewart with one brow raised.

"I'm surprised you were able to keep a secret with Chris in the know. I can usually count on him to spill the beans," said Grace.

"Actually, I've being communicating with Hanna since you told her you were coming home. She knew about our travel plans. As for Chris, I kept him at bay by telling Patrice to hide their suitcases until it was time to go. He actually had no idea. But once I told him where we were going, I bribed him with a new video game in case you did call before we got here, so he'd keep quiet."

Stewart and the kids had taken a flight from Knoxville to Jackson. They had a short layover in Memphis. Stewart told Grace that there was no way he was going to let her drive back home alone. She was actually relieved to know that she would have her regular chauffeur and the two best young people in the world with her on the drive back.

The children started in early with Chris saying, "Can we stay until Tuesday? I'm caught up on all of my schoolwork. Please."

"No, I have to be back by Monday to tie up some loose ends before Friday," said Grace.

Stewart told her in private that the children's teachers were aware of the upcoming surgery and said they could miss a few days if needed.

But Grace shook her head. "No, I don't want that to happen. I want them to keep a regular routine."

Grace, Stewart, and the kids went into the family room with the rest of the family where everyone sat and talked. The conversations swirled around questions about how the children were doing in school and what they would like as

Christmas gifts. Grace was about to tell Stewart about Samuel's wedding news, but Samuel said, "I picked them up at the airport. Hanna designated me the chauffeur for the day. So I told him on the ride over."

Stewart gave his congratulations again.

The subject of Grace's health never surfaced.

As the day progressed, everyone said their goodbyes. Grace and Stewart headed up to bed. Before they got to the bedroom door, Stewart whispered in Grace's ear, "We're telling the children tomorrow."

After the kids were tucked away in their room for the night, Grace asked, "Why here? I thought we were going to do that at home."

"Look, this is going to be a big adjustment for all of us. The children need to know and start preparing themselves along with you and me," said Stewart. "I also talked with Dr. Malloy, and he's still working out things with the department. Grace, he had to share your diagnosis with everyone because your absence affects your whole department. They're all figuring out how they can chip in and cover your caseload and your weeks that you were scheduled to be the attending physician on the hospital GI service. I told him that you were concerned about who knows, but baby, you're having surgery at your hospital. They're all going to know. So, please, let go of your pride. Accept help that's offered to you."

Grace sat and looked off in a blank stare as she let Stewart's words sink in. She said, "Okay. That makes sense I guess."

"Wow, that was easier than I thought it was going to be."

"Hanna and Sara have insisted that the kids will be fine. As for work, I'm okay with whatever. I've been making myself feel more sick with worry. So, are we going to tell them before or after church?" asked Grace.

"We should all talk before church, as early as possible."

As they lay in bed holding each other, Grace laid her head on Stewart's chest and tears began to fall. He pulled her chin up so that her face was directly facing his. He kissed her and said, "Superwoman, it's okay to need and accept help. We're going to get you through this as a family. You see how we are here for you right now, don't you? Well, get ready, because there is more of this kind of love to come."

She nodded.

"You've been there for so many people, so let someone be here for you," he went on to say.

They fell asleep and woke up in the same embrace.

CHAPTER 37

The sun's rays glistened through the slats of the plantation shutters, signaling to Grace and Stewart that it was time to get up. They went to the room where the children were sleeping. Grace sat on the bed where Christopher slept and Stewart sat on Patrice's bed.

Stewart said, "Rise and shine and give God the glory."

"Dad, what time is it? Why can't we sleep late?" asked Chris.

Patrice jumped up and said, "I'm up." But she laid back on the bed as she studied Grace's face. "What's happened?" she asked in a panicked voice.

"Well, guys, we actually came to be with Mommy because she's sick."

"Sick? She looks okay to me," said Chris.

"Mom, please tell me what's wrong," said Patrice worriedly.

Stewart was about to speak again, when Grace lifted her hand. "I'll answer, babe," she said. "So, I've been diagnosed with breast cancer and I'm going to have to have surgery on Friday. Then after that, I'll have to get chemotherapy and Auntie Shelley is going to be helping me with that. I'll be fairly sick, a lot, for a period of time, but ultimately, I believe I'll be fine."

Patrice began to cry. "Are you going to die?"

"I'm not planning on it," Grace said with a smile. She crossed over to Patrice's bed and embraced her as she brushed her hair back. "I'm going to really need you all to work with Daddy and Alice."

"I knew something bad had happened that day Daddy brought you home last week," said Patrice.

"Look, this is going to be challenging for me and tough on all of us. But I'm going to fight like hell to be here with you guys. You see, I have a few graduations, weddings, and grandchildren to see."

She pulled Patrice closer to her in an all-encompassing hug and told her that they all needed to say their own special prayers to God today at church about what they wanted Him to do for Mommy.

Stewart chimed in with, "Amen."

Grace couldn't tell if Christopher was in shock or just didn't understand it all as he stared off into space. Grace began to tear up as she looked over at him.

Stewart nodded to Grace and said, "Chris and I need to go to the bathroom and brush our teeth." He mouthed to Grace, "I'll try to get him talking."

"Can I talk to Auntie Shelley, Mom? I want to understand this better, and if you don't mind, can I do a Google search about cancer?" Patrice asked Grace.

Grace smiled as she rubbed Patrice's head. "I wouldn't expect anything less from you sweetheart, but let's get ready for church first."

Grace returned to her room and focused on her own Sunday attire. She pulled out a black, long-sleeved fitted dress; black pantyhose; and her black pumps. After showering, she pulled her dress over her head, smoothed it down over her waist and hips, brushed hair back into a ponytail, did a final once over in floor length mirror, and said, "That'll do."

She then made sure Patrice and Christopher were dressed and ready to go.

"You guys look like a million bucks," she said as they came through the doorway. Patrice wore her favorite navy-blue turtle neck sweater and plaid hunter green, red, and dark blue skirt. She wore navy blue tights and shoes. Both Stewart and Christopher looked respectable in brown suits with white shirts and gold ties.

When they came out to the kitchen, Hanna hurried everyone along after offering them a breakfast bar and coffee or juice for a quick breakfast.

"We're going out for brunch after church so we don't need to stuff ourselves now. Plus, Glen falls asleep in church if he eats a big breakfast first," she said.

Glen grunted, "It's not just the breakfast that makes me fall asleep. Sometimes the sermons are just boring. I'm sorry, y'all. No disrespect."

Hanna punched her husband. "Really, Glen, you need to stop that. God is listening to you."

Glen chuckled. "Well, if He's listening, then He has to have heard a few of the pastor's boring sermons. He needs to do something to rescue the sheep. I bet God is bored, too."

"Shame on you, Glen," said Hanna.

Grace focused on the children who were both solemn. She told Hanna, "Stewart and I talked with the children this morning."

Hanna turned to Patrice and Chris. "Listen, we are going to get through this. Your mom is the strongest person I know and if you all need to talk, you can call me anytime, day or night."

"Thanks, Auntie Hanna," said Patrice.

Chris remained silent.

While at church, Grace thought it was amazing that the pastor preached a sermon entitled, "Is There No Balm in Gilead?" She squeezed Stewart's hand as she remembered the Richard Smallwood song that he had played for her before her journey to Jackson.

Grace focused as the preacher said, "The balm of Gilead was an ointment that was expressed from a special plant grown in Gilead. It had the power to heal and soothe pain. It cured sickness. But, you see, today we don't have to find that plant, because Jesus is our balm. He's our healer. He wants to heal you in a way that modern medicine can't do."

Patrice leaned over. "Mom, I think God just gave us the sign."

Grace smiled and Stewart squeezed her hand as he heard Patrice's whisper. Grace took a deep breath and realized that since Stewart and the kids had arrived, she had stopped reflecting on the past. She appeared to be living in her now moment with the most important people in her life. *What love.*

After brunch, the Livingston family packed up the SUV and headed back to Tennessee. To Grace, the drive seemed shorter than before. She noticed that Chris stared out the window most of the way and wasn't talking.

"Are you okay, Christopher? You haven't said much since I told you what was going on with me this morning," said Grace.

"I'm all right. Daddy told me that I needed to be strong and I'm trying to do that."

Grace looked over at Stewart, who shrugged his shoulders, and then turned toward Chris in the back seat.

"Chris, it's okay to cry if you want. Being strong doesn't mean you can't talk about it or cry. I need you to talk to me. Part of me being okay is knowing that you're okay, buddy."

Christopher asked through tears, "Mom, is the moon going to be full tonight? I hope I get to look at it in my telescope. I miss doing that."

"I'm not sure, buddy, but I sure hope you get to see something good in your telescope when we get home. But, you know, it might be too late when we get there. We can always try to look tomorrow, though."

"Yes, ma'am. I love you, Mommy," Chris answered.

"I love you, too."

Patrice reached out for Chris and placed her arm around his shoulder. "I've got him, Mom."

Chris laid his head on his sister and cried.

Stewart said, "Son, I'm sorry if I confused you by saying what I did. We want you to cry if you need to. But we're all going to fight for Mommy to get better."

"Yes, sir," said Chris through his sniffles.

Grace turned to Patrice and mouthed, "Thank you," to which Patrice smiled. Her arm still around her brother, Patrice asked, "Mom, can I still go to the skating party that my school is having before Christmas break? It sounds like it's going to be a lot of fun. I'm going to bring my own skates because I don't like the ones at the skating rink."

Grace looked at Stewart with a smile as she said, "Absolutely, you can go."

Grace was comforted in knowing that Patrice seemed to be doing okay. Christopher's silence still concerned her, but she was happy that he had asked about his telescope.

Grace said to Stewart after they arrived home, "Thanks for being so wonderful. You were right, as usual. When I let go, I can see that God handles things much better than I."

CHAPTER 38

On Friday morning, Grace and Stewart pulled into the hospital parking lot at 5:30 a.m. as she was Dr. Huggin's the first surgical case of the day. After filling out admission papers, glancing over and signing the power of attorney and living will papers, Grace was called back to the pre-op area.

A staff member guided her to a bay that had her name written on a dry erase board attached to the wall above the bed. A name bracelet was placed on her left wrist. The nursing staff began to prep her for surgery.

A nurse placed an IV in her left hand and flushed in a bag of fluids. She had her vital signs taken by a different staff member who also gave her a tablet of Pepcid and Reglan to swallow with a sip of water.

At 6:35, Dr. Huggins pulled back her curtain at her pre-op bay and said, "Good morning, are you ready?"

"As ready as I can be."

Dr. Huggins dryly said, "Well, it's too late to back out now, anyway."

Grace noticed Stewart's frown. "Oh, Stewart, now you get to experience Dr. Huggins's award-winning humor. But you and I know that I'm a pretty good runner. I could get out of here if I needed to."

"Oh-kay," said Stewart.

After Dr. Huggins left the room, Grace reminded Stewart that Dr. Huggins had an excellent reputation for his surgical skills but had a terrible bedside manner and lacked a few social skills.

At 7:00 a.m., the nurses told Stewart they would have to kick him out. Right before he left, Stewart laid his hand on Grace's forehead and prayed a heartfelt prayer.

Tears began to flow as Grace heard him say, "Lord, you know how much I love this woman—but I know that you love her more. Your love for her is as wide as the ocean and as deep as the sea. I am trusting that You will guide the hands of the surgeon, the anesthesiologist, and the entire surgical team today, so that nothing bad happens to my baby. We are believing You for Grace's complete healing in advance of all that she will go through. Please let Your Spirit move in a mighty way today to cover her and restore her health. You are the Living Word and a healing rain in dry places. We need You, Lord. This family needs Grace. So, I ask You to show us Your grace and mercy right now, God, as only You can. It's in Your Mighty Name we pray, Amen."

They kissed and Stewart left the room.

Grace was rolled into a large operating room suite. She smiled as she thought about how the staff seemed so nice and professional. She recognized a lot of them but didn't know everyone by name. Grace was then moved over onto the operating table. She saw the anesthesiologist, Dr. Bentley, moving around the room checking gauges, intubation blades, and syringes.

He came over and said, "Hi, Grace, I know this has to be awkward for you, but you're in good hands. Dr. Huggins is the best 'breast guy' in town. I'll be here with you the whole time."

Dr. Bentley told her that he was about to give her a sedative, and she could close her eyes if she would like.

He said, "Pick out your favorite place or thought to focus on as you go to sleep."

"Okay, I'll do my best," said Grace before she started singing, *"Amazing grace! How sweet the sound that saved a wretch like me. I once was lost, but now am found; was blind, but now I see. Through many dangers, toils, and snares, I have already come; 'tis grace that brought me safe thus far, and grace will lead me home."*

After the surgery, Grace began the healing process and appreciated the fact that she was home.

AFTERWORD

Although this is a fictional story about Grace's challenge with breast cancer, the threat of breast cancer is real. My hope is that this book triggers a talk with your loved one about the need for breast cancer screening. Whether you feel afraid of being screened or simply feel you don't have the time or resources to get one done, I encourage you to push past whatever the obstacle may be and make it happen. Your life, or the life of someone you love, may be saved by doing one simple test.

Below are three interviews with real women who have faced issues like Grace's and were happy to share their stories with the author.

Robin L. Jones, M.D., is an obstetrician/gynecologist in Chicago, IL. She is currently on staff at Rush Presbyterian Hospital in Chicago. Robin was diagnosed with breast cancer in 2007 at the height of her career and had a recurrence in 2016.

Author: Can you tell me about how you were initially diagnosed and the impact that diagnosis had on your life?

Robin: *So, if we start with diagnosis, I was diagnosed because of a self-breast exam. I palpated a lump in my breast. You know, sometimes* *knowledge can be helpful or harmful. I knew that based on my age and the presence of the lump, that I most likely had breast cancer. Although, I was sincerely hoping it would be nothing more than a fibroadenoma or some other benign condition (in some ways much like Grace). So, as a result of that finding, I went to see my doctor.*

In regards to my recurrence, I have had an annual mammogram since my initial diagnosis but this time I wasn't told to leave as soon as I had been accustomed to doing with my previous exams. I felt there was something wrong. I was told that I had a mass in the other breast which was devastating. Having gone through chemotherapy and all of its rigors before, I was having a hard time deciding if I wanted to do it again.

Author: How did you select your physician?

Robin: *Being a physician, I was fortunate enough to be able to call a colleague of mine and ask whom she would recommend at her medical facility for a patient with possible breast cancer. I didn't tell her that I was the patient because I didn't want to alarm anyone. I also didn't choose the academic institution where I worked because I'm a very private person, and I needed the anonymity of just being a patient to get the care I needed. After selecting a breast surgeon based on my colleague's recommendation and doing some of my own research, I had a breast biopsy done and a week later returned to the doctor's office to review my biopsy results. I was told that it was cancer then, though I kind of knew in my heart that it was already. The interesting thing is that my colleague who recommended the breast surgeon is married to the physician who ended up ultimately being my oncologist. He and I had never met prior to this encounter. I chose the same team for my second surgery and for chemotherapy.*

Author: At any point did you ask, "Am I going to die?"

Robin: *I was terrified and had lots of things going through my head. But, in all honesty, I think the hardest thing for me was how I was going* *to tell my family. It was harder than telling myself that I have breast cancer and that I could die. I told my family in stages. My father was the first one that I told when I found the lump in my breast. I also asked him to go with me for the biopsy and to the appointment to get my final pathology results. The next person that I told was my mother, after I found out that it was indeed cancer. I told my sister who lives in Chicago next. My youngest sister was living in a different state with her family at the time, and she was pregnant with twins. I didn't want to just call her on the phone with this type of information; so, I took a flight to see her and told her in person. Each of those conversations was the hardest thing for me around the time of my diagnosis because family is everything to me. You can't put a price on family. The love that was shown during that time was priceless. I was vulnerable because in many ways I felt helpless during the times I needed help from others. I was not accustomed to having someone take care of me. Being a very private person, it was awkward to have people living and staying with me to take care of me. It was just difficult. It was huge for me. But the love they showed to me. You can't put a price on it.*

Author: Did you ask, "Why me, God?"

Robin: *I didn't ask that because there is never a good answer to that question. It's not that I was so confident that He would make a way for me. But what I did know is that God loved me. And because of His love, I didn't believe He would just let this haphazardly happen to me. This may sound crazy, but I believe I was chosen for this. Although I didn't understand the "why," I knew it wasn't by chance, either. I don't believe God operates like that. Even though I didn't understand things, I knew that He loved me and that He doesn't make any mistakes. Given that, I could accept it. I decided to look at it as, He chose me because I was special. I quoted a lot of Scripture during that time.*

Also, another ironic thing is that not long after I shared my diagnosis with one of my childhood friends, she ended up having three other friends receive the same diagnosis. God allowed me to be a testimony to those other women who ended up going through the same struggle that I had been through. They happened to be three professional women. Resources were not an issue for them or me, like getting the mammogram was not my concern and seeing a physician routinely was not the issue. This disease has no respecter of person.

Author: Being a physician, did you feel you had an advantage because you understood the literature and studies that were published about breast cancer research and treatment?

Robin: *I chose not to get on the internet and search for information and read what was out there. I had an aunt who gave me lots of information that she had gathered out of concern, but I chose not to read it. I didn't need too much information to confuse me. I see my life as a journey and all of those studies, which can scare you to death, were not what I needed to see or read. I just prayed and had family and friends praying for me. I was terrified, of course. But I felt that being a child of God gave me a leg up.*

Author: How did you and your oncologist communicate about your treatment options and what you could expect from the chemotherapy?

Robin: *As I mentioned earlier, my colleague's husband ended up being my oncologist, and she told me that I could call him whenever I needed him. I didn't plan to be a "stalker" patient, but I saw it as another blessing from God that He had essentially given me open access to my doctor. I know that most patients aren't afforded that type of connection to their physician.*

Also, I was told that most patients traditionally had surgery and then chemotherapy. I asked why surgery had to be done first. My oncologist was open to me asking questions and after further discussion, we decided to do chemotherapy first and then surgery. I chose this route because I am the sole breadwinner, and as a single woman, I was trying to not have too much time off work. I was blessed because I only missed a couple of days due to a viral illness during my chemo. I continued to see patients daily. I did my chemo on Fridays which allowed me to have the weekends to recover. The chemotherapy shrank the tumor so much during treatment that they had to put a marker on the site of the tumor so that the surgeon could excise the right area. I did not agree to a lymph node dissection because of concerns about lymphedema, but I did undergo radiation to my axilla which is the area where they would have dissected the lymph nodes. I did things somewhat nontraditionally, but I had to do what I felt was right for me. I was able to ask pertinent questions about how my treatment plan would be altered based on the order in which the treatments were done and what the findings may or may not reveal. Regarding the issue of prognosis, I felt God already knew what that was, so I was okay with whatever He had planned out for me.

During my recurrence, I had a whole new level of stress in my life as my father was terminally ill and I felt more alone this time. My Dad had been there with me when I was given my initial diagnosis but I couldn't really share it with him this time. I couldn't burden him. I depended more on my sisters, my mother, and you to be a support system. I am still on the journey this time and am seeking God for what He would have me to ultimately do. I did have surgery and took more chemotherapy but I have refocused on what is important in my life, God's love, my family, and friends.

Mrs. Carol Garrett is the sister of the author and one of the faces on the cover of this book. Carol is currently a retired insurance underwriter for BCBS of MS. She was diagnosed with breast cancer in 2007.

Author: When you were diagnosed, what came to mind for you after receiving such devastating news?

Carol: *Actually, when I was diagnosed, my first question was about death.*

Author: Did you ask that question of the doctor or of God? Or was that just something you contemplated to yourself?

Carol: *My first conversation was really with God. I had been told my mammograms had been abnormal several times in the past, because I had fibrocystic breast disease. The fibrocystic breast lesions caused things to look suspicious on my mammograms often. I had grown accustomed to having further testing done after my mammogram. So, I wasn't too worried. However, on this occasion, I had been called back in for a special sonogram of my breast. A new twist for me was when they asked me to wait in a room in which I had never done before after one of those tests.*

After having the test, a physician whom I had never met before entered the room and introduced herself as a breast surgeon. She told me that based on her professional experience with breast cancer and given the abnormal findings seen on my mammogram and ultrasound that she believed I had breast cancer. She said she was prepared to do a biopsy on my breast at that moment and then we would have to wait on the path report to confirm the diagnosis, but she was almost 100% positive that it was cancer. I was floored. She seemed so sure when she made that statement. I was totally unprepared because I had just taken a work break to come for an ultrasound. It had never crossed my mind that a biopsy would be performed on that day. I had no family or friends with me at that moment. Looking back, I realize that I had a right to say, Hold up—I need my family with me for the biopsy, but I was so afraid and caught off guard that I just answered yes out of fear.

After I agreed to have the biopsy and had it performed, my fear began to grow even more. I immediately began to tear up and cry after the surgeon left the room. I went to my car in the parking lot of the hospital and sat there for about an hour and a half. I cried out to God and asked

Him if this was the end for me. I said to Him that if this was my death sentence, then I guess I'd have to accept it. I didn't understand it, but I knew I had to accept it. I asked God to help me through the process, the pain, and all that I was going to suffer. I asked Him to just please be there with me through it all. I knew that I already had a place with my Father in Heaven, so that part didn't really scare me. I had even started imagining that part of my transition while sitting there in the parking lot.

But there were a lot of things on this side, the earthly side, that bothered me. There were things that I had wanted to do in my life that I felt I might not ever get to do. I told God that I would miss my children and my family, but please just take care of them for me, if I can't be there to see them grow up. So, in essence, at the time of being told that diagnosis, I immediately focused on—am I about to die? It was a lonely place for me at that time because I didn't have anyone with me. Again, I had just taken a break from work to run in and get a test done.

After I cried for a while, then my next question to myself was, I wonder how they are going to treat this? And then my mind went to— how far gone was this thing, and would they be able to cure it? I wasn't up on the research or anything like that. So, I didn't know much about it. I had relatives who had both lived and died with breast cancer and had been acquainted with several women who had died from breast cancer. They may not have died immediately after their diagnosis, but a few years down the road, they died from the disease.

So, my first question was, will I die? And my next question was about the cure. But for me, my last question for God was, why me? I asked myself what I had done that I deserved this type of illness—this death sentence. You have to understand, I don't have medical knowledge at my fingertips. I didn't know all of the questions to ask. I was just stunned and felt alone.

Initially feeling defeated while sitting in the parking lot, I decided to just go home. But then something came over me. I felt I had a chance of not having cancer. I remembered that once before I had been told that I had an abnormal spot on my mammogram and had to have a biopsy. That biopsy was benign. So, in my mind, I felt that I had put everything out there to God, and I was going to be okay. I felt like He had protected me before—why wouldn't He do that now? So, I decided to go back to work. I decided to wait on the path report.

But, as fate would have it, the surgeon was right, and not only did I have cancer in the breast that she biopsied, but I also had cancer in the other breast. I elected to have a bilateral mastectomy because the MRI scan of my breast done prior to surgery showed an irregularity in the other breast. I was told that we could just watch that area and cross the road of removal of that breast later if we needed to do so. As I stated earlier, I was glad I made the decision to have a bilateral mastectomy because there was cancer in both breasts.

Author: So, were you doing monthly self-exams at home? Don't be afraid to answer because, unfortunately, so many women don't.

Carol: *I didn't. Since I have the fibrocystic breasts, it was difficult for me to tell one lump from another. I had been to the doctor many times when I thought I felt something in the past, but it always turned out to be nothing, and I would be told that I just have "lumpy breasts."*

Author: After you saw your breast surgeon and your oncologist, how did you all talk about what to expect after surgery and from the effects of chemotherapy?

Carol: *I initially met with the breast surgeon, and she was very thorough, going through all of my surgical options. But in all honesty, I was still in a fog after receiving my diagnosis. So, although she was thorough, I'm not sure how much I understood. The surgeon actually helped me determine who my oncologist would be, as well. And it helped having you along with me, with your medical knowledge, as well as my* *husband and my children. However, the surgeon felt it was most important for both me and my husband to understand everything that was going to take place. I appreciated her thoroughness.*

After surgery, when I met with my oncologist, I didn't really know the questions to ask. He explained to me my cancer type. He said that I actually had a fairly low-grade type of cancer which meant that I didn't have to have more aggressive forms of chemotherapy. The intravenous medications I received did make me very sick. My white blood cell count dropped, and I had to have medication to correct that. I developed neuropathy in my hands and feet and started having leg pains that I had never had before. I ultimately had a little hair loss, which was unusual according to the nursing staff. My oncologist was very supportive throughout the entire process. I would like to say that I had read a lot of information about breast cancer treatment, but I didn't before I had to get started with my therapy. I did talk over everything for my family and I explained to them that I felt comfortable with what my oncologist was saying. So, I chose to move forward with his treatment plan.

Author: At any point, did you have concerns about who would be there for you during your day-to-day care?

Carol: *I did to some extent. My husband was supportive but had a very busy work schedule. I had two sisters who were living in the same city with me, but they were both working jobs that took them out of town from early morning to the late evening. So, I didn't expect them to lose time from their jobs to take me for my chemotherapy appointments. And you lived in another state and had a busy schedule of your own and couldn't be there for my day-to-day care. I did have some assistance from one of my sisters-in-law which I greatly appreciated, as well as our cousin, Lana, who would take me to my chemotherapy appointments. I really felt I needed female support to help me with some of my personal needs, but that was not always available.*

Patricia Elliot, M.D., is a former obstetrician/gynecologist in Montgomery, AL. She was in private practice and was diagnosed with stage 1 breast cancer in 2014. Pat continued to work a full schedule and remained determined through her time of diagnosis.

Author: So, Pat, can you tell me how you felt when you were diagnosed with breast cancer and actually how your diagnosis was made?

Pat: *I found my lump doing a breast self-exam. I have fibrocystic breast and am used to feeling lumps, but this one felt different. So, when I got the diagnosis, initially my concern was that I had done this to myself, having taken unopposed estrogen for over 14 years. But I then found out that I had triple negative breast cancer, grade III, on my pathology which means that the estrogen had not played a role. I was going to get it, anyway. So, then I was glad that I hadn't denied myself estrogen for all those years and had to deal with menopausal symptoms without taking estrogen.*

Author: Did the "why me" question arise for you?

Pat: *I never said "why me." But what I did it say was "let me find out as much about this process as I can." I immediately started reading about it. I realized I had one of the worst grades of breast cancer that you could have. So, I knew right away that I would have a mastectomy. So, I called a friend who's a surgeon and I told him that I wanted to have my surgery as soon as possible along with a sentinel node biopsy. The surgeon asked me if I wanted to talk about some conservative types of therapy first. I told him no because I needed to know the extent of my disease. I explained that I had to figure out my life plan as soon as possible.*

Author: It's really interesting that you were fairly certain about how you wanted your cared managed, because everybody seems to be different in their approach to this disease. Would you agree with that people approach management differently?

Pat: *I believe that this is a very individual approach when it comes to treatment for breast cancer. I think more women should be empowered to know that they have options and have the right to ask questions before proceeding. I want women to know that, sure, it's scary when someone tells you that you have cancer, but take a deep breath, step back, and look at the whole picture. The patient needs to listen to all the options and then go home and think about it. You have to make the decision that's right for you.*

I chose my oncologist based on the fact that he had a history of cancer himself and understood what chemotherapy would be like. I can honestly say that I have an aversion of sorts to chemotherapy. So, it was an uphill battle for me and my oncologist to come to an agreement about the type of chemotherapy. Initially I was told I would need Adriamycin, Cytoxan and Taxol. I quickly vetoed Adriamycin because of its cardiac toxicity. I was concerned about my heart function, given the fact that Adriamycin has cardiomyopathy as a known risk factor. I agreed to try Cytoxan and Taxol. But I had almost made up in my mind that I was not going to try chemotherapy. I asked what was my ten-year survival rate with and without chemotherapy. I was given a number somewhere around 78% without chemotherapy, and it only increased by about 6% to 84% with chemotherapy. I decided I would try chemotherapy primarily because I have a new grand baby that I wanted to see grow up.

But I knew I was not happy with the thought of chemotherapy. I took one "helping"—the way I like to think of it—of chemotherapy and became extremely ill. I had a severe reaction to the pretreatment steroids. I developed a facial droop. They actually thought I had a TIA or a stroke. My workup for stroke was negative. It was decided that I just had a severe reaction to the steroids. But after I recovered somewhat, I started the chemotherapy on a Friday. By Tuesday of the following week, I started having abdominal pain. I thought it would go away and was able to operate that day. But by Wednesday night, I became violently ill. I had some of the worst of abdominal pain I had ever had in my life. By the time I saw the oncologist on Thursday, my white blood cell count was extremely low, and they felt I might have had an infection. I had to go to the cancer center daily for antibiotics.

After that first dose of chemotherapy, I decided I would not do it again. My oncologist tried to persuade me to not respond so quickly, but I explained that I had made up my mind that I couldn't and wouldn't do it anymore. My nail beds turned dark within a week and my hair fell out within one week. That didn't bother me as much as seeing my white blood cell count drop so low. I had seen my best friend die from the side effects of chemotherapy for ovarian cancer eighteen years prior and I didn't want that to happen to me. And I'm at peace and happy with my decision.

Author: Did you have concerns about lymphedema like many women do? Was radiation ever an option for your treatment?

Pat: *As a gyn surgeon, I too had concerns about the possibility of lymphedema. But I thought it was less likely with just doing a sentinel node biopsy. However, I was a little dismayed when I found out that the surgeon took it upon himself to take out more lymph nodes than we had agreed upon. Really, I think he thought he was protecting me and doing the right thing. But I was somewhat upset with the fact that he didn't trust what I was saying to him. I explained to him that I'm a golfer, and I frequently have to wear sleeveless shirts. And I didn't want to deal with lymphedema. I do have a little bit of lymphedema on the back of my arm, but I think that it can be corrected cosmetically. I also chose to not have reconstructive surgery at the time of my surgery because I didn't want to be under anesthesia too long. Realizing that I had a very aggressive lesion and if it looked like I absolutely needed to have chemotherapy, I didn't* *want recovery from surgery to be an issue for holding up my chemo. I felt that reconstructive surgery could happen later, if I chose to do so.*

Regarding radiation, I requested radiation or at least inquired about it. I was told that I didn't need it because I had clean margins.

BREAST CANCER FACTS

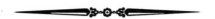

- Cancer is a disease in which cells become abnormal and rapidly duplicate themselves. With breast cancer, the cancer begins in cells that make up the breasts—usually in the tubes that carry milk to the nipple or the glands that make milk.

- About 1 in 8 U.S. women—a little more than 12%—will develop invasive breast cancer over the course of her lifetime.

- In 2014, an estimated 232,670 new cases of invasive breast cancer were expected to be diagnosed, along with 62,570 new cases of non-invasive breast cancer (also known as carcinoma in situ). With an estimated 40,160 deaths to occur in 2017, breast cancer is the second leading cause of death among women in the US. Although there has been a decrease in death rates since 1989, with larger decreases in women under 50. These may be the result of treatment advancements, earlier detection through screening, and increased awareness. Over the past several years, disagreement has arisen over the age a patient should initiate routine screening with the United States Preventive Services Task Force recommending that average risk women undergo routine screening biennially at age 50. The most important matter is that routine screening be performed.

- For women in the United States, breast cancer death rates are higher than death rates for any other type of cancer, besides lung cancer.

- White women are slightly more likely to develop breast cancer than African-American women. However, breast cancer is more common in African-American women under 45 than white women in the same age bracket. Overall, African-American women are more likely to die of breast cancer. In contrast to incidence, breast cancer death rates are higher among black women than white women in every state, with rates in some states (e.g., Louisiana and Mississippi) as much as 60% higher. Among women 20 – 49 years of age, the Black to White disparity in breast cancer mortality is the largest disparity among cancer-specific disease and has widened over the past 30 years. Asian, Hispanic, and Native-American women have a lower risk of developing and dying from breast cancer.

- As of 2014, there were more than 2.8 million women with a history of breast cancer in the U.S. This figure includes women currently being treated and women who have finished treatment.

- A woman's risk of breast cancer approximately doubles if she has a first-degree relative (mother, sister, or daughter) who has been diagnosed with breast cancer.

- Less than 15% of women who get breast cancer have a family member who has been diagnosed with it.

- About 5-10% of breast cancers are thought to be caused by inherited gene mutations (abnormal changes passed through families).

- The most significant risk factors for breast cancer are gender (being a woman) and age (growing older).

- The role of breast self-examination (BSE) remains controversial but most gynecologists suggest that average-risk women not perform BSE. Several studies have shown lack of benefit and a higher rate of breast biopsy that shows benign disease with routine BSE.

- Women who nonetheless choose to perform BSE should receive careful instruction to differentiate normal tissue from suspicious lumps and understand that BSE is an adjunct, but not a substitute, for mammography.

- Women should be encouraged to bring abnormal breast findings promptly to the attention of their physician.

- Some women want to do exams on their own breasts. No study has shown that breast self-exams lower the risk of dying from breast cancer. Still, if you decide to do breast self-exams, make sure you know how to do them the right way.

RESOURCES

For more information about breast cancer, call womenshealth.gov at 800-994-9662 (TDD: 888-220-5446) or contact the following organizations:

- **American Cancer Society**
  800-227-2345
- **National Breast and Cervical Cancer Early Detection Program**
  800-232-4636
- **National Cancer Institute, NIH, HHS**
  800-422-6237
- **Susan G. Komen for the Cure**
  877-465-6636
- **Y-ME National Breast Cancer Organization**
  800-221-2141
- **US Preventive Services Task Force**
  Screening for breast cancer: U.S. Preventive Services Task Force recommendation statement. Ann Intern Med 2009; 151:716.
- **World Health Organization**
  Breast cancer: prevention and control; 2015.
  http://www.who.int/cancer/detection/breastcancer/en/

Share this information!

DISCUSSION QUESTIONS

In the book, Grace is a medical professional who had her life changed suddenly by a cancer diagnosis. In spite of her medical knowledge, she didn't initially identify the warning signs of breast cancer. This small workbook asks questions that prompt reflection and foresight.

1) What would you do at the first recognition of a lump in your breast, having had a normal mammogram previously?

_____

_____

_____

_____

_____

2) Do you perform breast self-exams at home? Would you feel better and more secure doing those exams if you were taught to perform them properly?

_____

_____

_____

_____

_____

3) What do you think is an appropriate response to pain or discharge from one of your breasts? Whom do you consult about your concerns? When?

_____

_____

_____

_____

_____

4) Grace had a hard time dealing with how to communicate her diagnosis to her family. She later realized that she had carried a lot of undue stress in her attempt to manage everyone else's response to her diagnosis. How would or could you tell a spouse or significant other?

_____

_____

_____

_____

_____

5) Thinking about your mortality can be more difficult as a parent. How would or could you tell your children about a breast cancer diagnosis?

_____

_____

_____

_____

_____

6) Write down your thoughts on how you could or would tell your siblings or parents.

_____

_____

_____

_____

_____

7) Do you believe family support plays a role in physical and mental healing, and if so, how?

_____

_____

_____

_____

_____

8) Do you believe that faith in a power greater than oneself plays a role in the mental and emotional health of an individual after a cancer diagnosis? If so, how?

_____

_____

_____

_____

_____

9) Has this book caused you to see the power of personal reflection during a time of crisis, whether it is cancer or another type of crisis? If so, how?

_____

_____

_____

_____

_____

10) Grace references "home" throughout the story. What do you think she meant by the term? What comes to mind when you think of "home"?

_____

_____

_____

ACKNOWLEDGMENTS

To all of the special people who have taken this journey with me, I extend heartfelt gratitude.

Mrs. Janice Sykes-Rogers, for your encouragement and guidance. You are a rare and unique jewel.

Drs. Terry and Jevonnah Ellison, for rekindling the fire in me to complete this project and the spiritual support throughout the process.

Ms. Janelle Aygeman, for your honest review of my first version of this book and direction to see it to completion.

Mrs. Lana Nicks, for your mentoring throughout my life and on this project, in particular.

Mrs. Barbara Davis, kudos for your beautiful painting that is now the cover of this book.

The Writer's Ally staff, thanks for your direction and patience with a burgeoning writer.

Ms. Renita Bryant and The Mynd Matters Publishing team, for their help in pushing me across the finish line.

Lastly, to all of my family and friends who have been a support to me in so many ways, you have my sincere gratitude and love.